Treacherous

Livelihoods

Roberta Cava

Treacherous Livelihoods

Roberta Cava

Published by Cava Consulting

cavaconsulting@ozemail.com.au

Discover other titles by Roberta Cava at

www.dealingwithdifficultpeople.info

National Library of Australia

Cataloguing-in-publication data:

ISBN 978-0648934660

This is a book of fiction. All the characters and events portrayed in this novel are either products of the author's imagination or are used fictitiously.

BOOKS BY ROBERTA CAVA

All can be purchased from Amazon Books

Non-Fiction

Dealing with Difficult People
(International best-seller since 1990 with 24 publishers – in 18 languages in over 100 countries)
Dealing with Difficult Situations – at Work and at Home
Dealing with Difficult Spouses and Children
Dealing with Difficult Relatives and In-Laws
Dealing with Domestic Violence and Child Abuse
Dealing with School Bullying
Dealing with Workplace Bullying
Retirement Village Bullies
Keeping Our Children Safe
Just say no
What am I going to do with the rest of my life?
Interpersonal Communication at Work
Change? Not me!
Creative Problem-Solving & Decision-Making
Customer Service that Works
Teambuilding
Before tying the knot
How Women can advance in business
Survival Skills for Supervisors and Managers
Human Resources at its Best!
Human Resources Policies and Procedures - Australia
Employee Handbook
Easy Come – Hard to go – The Art of Hiring, Disciplining and Firing Employees
Time and Stress – Today's silent killers
Take Command of your Future – Make things Happen
Belly Laughs for All! – Volumes 1 to 6
Wisdom of the World! The happy, sad & wise things in life!
The Presenter

Covid-19 200 Days – Facts and Fun
Covid-19 200-400 Days – Facts and Fun

Fiction

That Something Special
Something Missing
I can do it! The sky's the limit!
Twists and Turns
Treacherous Livelihoods
Life Gets Complicated
Life Goes On
Life Gets Better
Life in Isolation

Chapter 1

Thirty-nine-year-old Becky Wilson had met her husband Detective Dan Jeffries when he was still a Sergeant with the Edmonton Police Services. He'd been the first on site when Becky phoned the station to report that she'd just killed a man. She had walked in on a man in the process of raping her twelve-year-old daughter Sandy. She'd put her hands under the intruder's chin and pulled with all her might to get him off her daughter, killing him instantly when she broke his neck.

Dan became a good friend to both Becky and her daughter Sandy, and their friendship developed into love. He had little contact with her son Ken who was working in Edson. During a meal he'd shared with Becky, he explained that he was going to be doing a talk at Sandy's elementary school about the dangers of the new synthetic drugs and cyber bullying. He was also going to warn them about the possibility that going onto chat rooms on the internet could make them targets for podophiles.

As he talked to Becky, he explained that the police force would only be able to speak to the elementary students, but unfortunately didn't have enough manpower to do talks to the junior and senior high school students or colleges and universities. Becky suggested that she might be able to help him out. She was a member of the local Crime Stoppers volunteer group and wondered if the police department would like some of their volunteers to do the talks to the junior and senior high school students.

Dan promised to ask his police chief to see if this would be approved and was given the go-ahead for the volunteers to do the talks to the junior and senior high school students. Over the next year, Becky and a few other Crime Stoppers volunteers were able to speak to the sixty-three junior high schools and planned to speak to the seventy-five high schools the next year.

Dan and Becky fell in love and soon moved in together. When it became necessary for Dan's two-year-old son Mike to move in with them, they bought a bigger home. Dan's ex-wife Emily had been paralysed from the waist down when her car swerved off the road as she was driving her car on slippery winter roads. Everyone knew that she was lucky to come out of the accident alive.

Becky's daughter Sandy and little Mike got along well, and she loved having a little brother to care for. She was a very nurturing child and was good with him.

Dan and Becky enjoyed living together and decided to get married at the end of June. Sandy, Ken, and little Mike all took part in the ceremony.

They had not been home from their honeymoon long when Becky realized that she was pregnant. She agonized over whether Dan would be pleased or not. Her son Ken was now twenty and her daughter Sandy was thirteen, so there would be them to consider as well as Dan's son Mike who was now three. Their family would be well spaced out.

'Dan, I need to talk to you about something,' she started quietly. 'I don't know how you will feel about what I have to say.'

'Okay honey, what do you want to discuss?' He wondered if she needed his advice on something that was happening at work; was she ill; was there some problem in their marriage? He looked at her with a worried look on his face.

'Well, I've been meaning to talk to you about this for two weeks now,' she said, not really wanting to discuss the issue, but knowing she had to, 'and couldn't seem to find the right time to do so.'

He felt she was delaying what she had to say and could see she was quite emotional. 'You have me worried. Please tell me what you have to say,' he said as he took her hand in his.

'Well... I don't know how to tell you this or how you will feel about this, but I'm pregnant,' she winced as she said the last few words.

His eyes lit up, 'Are you sure?' he asked.

'Yep, I did the drugstore test yesterday and saw my GP today. You're going to be a daddy in about seven months' time.' She didn't know how he would feel about this revelation, because after all she'd just turned thirty-nine, rather late to have a child and her son was now almost twenty. And the reason she and her ex-husband Shane had adopted Sandy was because she'd had multiple miscarriages, so knew there was a good possibility that she could lose this one as well.

'Yahoo,' Dan all but shouted, and then put his hand over his mouth looking towards their bedroom door wondering if the children had heard him. 'I didn't think I'd have a chance of having another child. I'm over the moon that we can have a baby we're both part of. Oh honey, I'm so happy.'

Becky was very relieved. She'd been very concerned about her news and didn't know how he would feel especially so soon after their marriage.

'How do you feel about having another baby?' he asked.

'A bit scared. I know the chance of having pregnancy problems is much higher at my age, but my GP assured me that because of advanced medicine, he'll be able to monitor my pregnancy better than they could when I was having all those miscarriages before Shane and I adopted Sandy. He has advised me to stop going into the publishing office, and if I'm still editing books, to do it at home where I can rest if I'm tired. He doesn't want me to overdo it at all. He also suggested that I hire someone to do the heavy housework like vacuuming, making beds or anything else that will strain me. Can we afford for me to work part-time and have help with the housework? Can we make it on less money?'

'With my new promotion to detective, I'm sure we'll manage fine,' he assured her.

The next day at work, Becky spoke to her boss, Jim Stevens and got his permission to work out of her home.

'You're my best editor and it won't matter whether you're working from home or here in the office. Just keep receipts for any office expenses you have. I think you should have a business phone, so you can liaise with the authors and the office via phone and internet. We'll pay for that as well.'

He continued, 'Instead of being on a set salary, we could pay you according to the number of pages in a book you edit. How does that sound to you?'

'I like that idea and I won't feel I have to put in a full eight hours a day. If I'm tired, I can take it easy and work fewer hours in a day,' she agreed.

After interviewing several women, they hired Irma to be their housekeeper to work three days a week. Irma cooked their meals, did their laundry and their shopping. As Becky entered the second month of her pregnancy, she became so nauseated, that she could barely get out of bed. She was glad that she could take the odd day off to indulge herself and not feel pressured to keep working.

Sandy was over the moon that her mother was going to have a baby and sympathized with her when she was so nauseous. She brought her crackers and herbal teas that seemed to help her and couldn't do enough for her mother. The only thing she missed was that her mother couldn't go to the school soccer games she played in. She was an excellent soccer player but didn't spend as much time playing the game as she used to. now that she was in junior high. Instead, she'd become serious about practicing skateboarding at her local community centre with her boyfriend Jason Marcowitz. Jason was two years older than Sandy, but they'd been close friends for over two years. He was an excellent skateboarder and had won several contests. He also coached Sandy and she became very good at the sport.

Chapter 2

Dan, Becky and Sandy were watching a television commercial when Dan leaned forward and pointing to the little boy in the advertisement and said, 'I know him! That's Sergeant Denise Flannigan's five-year-old son Grady. She told me a few weeks ago that Grady had been at a birthday party held at McDonald's and a man approached the mother of the birthday boy to ask who Grady was and could he have the contact details for his parents. Rather than do that, the mother had asked him to give her a business card and she would have Grady's parents call him.'

'Denise told me that his business card said that he worked for a modelling agency. When she phoned the number on the card the man asked her whether he could come to speak with her about letting her son be a model for commercials. During his visit he also asked whether the boy's seven-year-old sister Kali could audition as well. Denise talked it over with her husband and children and they agreed to try it.'

He leaned forward as he said, 'As you saw from the commercial, Grady has bright red curly hair, an angelic face with no freckles and the most beautiful brown eyes. His sister has long blond hair and is also as cute as a button, so she'll likely be in commercials as well. I must talk to Denise at work tomorrow,' he added.

'He is awfully cute,' admitted Sandy.

'He's also an extremely well-behaved little boy who's completely unaware of how cute he is. I'm sure he'll do well as a model for commercials.'

The next day Dan tapped Denise Flannigan on the shoulder and congratulated her on the appearance of her son in the commercial. 'He certainly is a cute little guy,' he added as he noted the bright red blush on Denise's cheeks.

'I was a bit leery about letting him do it, but they kept telling me that he was exactly the kind of boy they were looking for. I hope it doesn't go to his head that he's now been on television. I can only imagine what will be happening today at his kindergarten class.'

'He'll be okay. When I met him that one time, I was impressed with what a well-behaved boy he is,' added Dan.

Then he changed the topic, 'Are you working on a case?'

'Yes, I am,' she said, 'It's not one I like to do because it hits too close to home. A mother took her six-year-old daughter to their doctor to treat an ongoing bladder infection. The doctor did a thorough examination and had to inform the mother that the child had damage to her vagina and had likely been raped. The mother was devastated. The doctor asked who could have done that to her. The mother said the only man that was in her life now that she was a single mother was her brother Walter. The doctor said she had to report the incident. She called us and arranged for me and a child counsellor to speak with the child. The counsellor came out of the room and showed us a picture the child had drawn that showed a small figure and a big one that appeared to have a full erection. The little girl said that Uncle Walter had a little leg sticking straight out in front of him.

I'm here to get a warrant for his arrest. What a world we live in!' she ended with a sigh.

'You've got that right,' Dan agreed.

The next time he saw Denise, she was quite upset, 'That bastard got off and didn't receive a sentence because of a technicality in the law. The thought of that animal on the loose is making me lose sleep. He's been warned not to come near his niece, or he'll be put in jail. At least the little girl has some protection, and the mother has completely disowned her brother.'

A few weeks later, Dan received a call to investigate a missing child. A young child had been playing in the school playground and had not come in after recess. He was only five and in kindergarten. A police search of the neighbourhood was begun. When Dan arrived at the school, he was surprised to see Denise Flannigan there in tears. 'What happened?' he asked.

'My son Grady is missing!' she sobbed. 'He's the child who's missing. They suspect that he's been kidnapped.'

'I've been told to speak with his teacher and the principal. Do you want to come with me?' he asked.

'Yes, please. I know I can't be part of the investigation, but he is my son. He has to watch what he eats – can't eat gluten or milk products.' she sobbed.

The teacher and principal of the school were both in tears. Grady's teacher said, 'Grady would never wander off. In many ways Grady is a timid boy and would have stayed with his classmates.'

'Did anyone see him leave?' Dan asked.

'I spoke with his classmates, but they were all playing football, so weren't paying any attention to Grady. Sorry,' his teacher replied.

Dan spoke with several other children and the adults on duty at the playground when he disappeared. He then went back to the police station to arrange for a wider police search for the child. He suggested that Denise go home to see if he had somehow gone home. She promised to call him when she got home. She did so, and he knew right away from her tone of voice that Grady wasn't there.

'Why don't you stay home. I can tell your senior officer what's happened and I'm sure he'll understand why you can't come in today,' he suggested.

'I want to come in, so I'll be kept informed about the progress of the police search. I've asked my neighbour to come over to my home to watch for Grady, so I don't have to stay here,' she said emphatically, and Dan knew that he had to accept her decision.

The next few days were agonising for the entire police force knowing that one of their officer's children had likely been kidnapped. They expected to receive a ransom note, but none arrived. Denise and her family were so strung out that her husband Blaine and seven-year-old daughter Kali kept waking up during the night thinking they heard him at the door of their home. They finally cuddled together in the parent's king-sized bed, but all of them were walking zombies by the third day.

The afternoon of the third day, an excited woman called 911, the emergency number and said, 'I think I've got the little boy who was kidnapped. Could you come and get him?'

The police officer obtained the elderly woman's address and phone number, and Dan was informed of the phone call. Then the officer phoned Denise to tell her about the phone call he cautioned. 'Don't get your hopes up. The woman sounded very old and could possibly be confused.'

'I'm on my way!' said Denise as she grabbed her purse and quickly phoned her husband Blaine at work about the call.

Denise and Dan arrived at the same time and Denise knew that Dan had to be the first on the scene. It was agony waiting in her car, but the agony was over within minutes when Dan came to her car carrying Grady.

Grady reached for his mother and started crying. He was still wearing the clothes he'd been wearing when he went missing, his hair was dirty and pasted to his head and he had a big bruise on his cheekbone.

'We have to take him to the hospital to be checked out,' Dan advised. Denise knew that they would be required to do a rape test to see whether he'd been sexually abused. Denise explained to Grady what they were going to do.

'I want to go home!' he wailed.

'You'll be going home real soon. But first we have to take you to the hospital to see if you're all right.'

'Okay Mom,' he said as he snuggled down in her arms.

Dan called ahead to the hospital and advised Blaine where to meet them. Besides informing the hospital about the boy's condition, he also phoned Family Services to have a trained child psychologist available to speak to Grady. He warned Denise and Blaine, 'Don't ask him any questions. We'll have a counsellor interview him. The counsellor will know what questions to ask, so the child won't get confused.'

When the physical and psychological tests had been completed, the counsellor called Denise and Blaine into a conference room. Dan and the examining doctor were already there.

The counsellor began as she read her notes, 'Grady says he was playing with a toy at the side of the school grounds when a man asked him whether he had seen his puppy. The man explained that the puppy was a very little one and was probably frightened. He asked Grady to help him look for it. Grady said he took his hand and was lifted over the playground fence. At this point in the interview Grady looked at the counsellor and stated, 'I wasn't supposed to do that was I? Mommy has always told me not to go with strangers, but I wanted to help him find his puppy.'

When asked what happened next, Grady started to cry and said, 'The man put some plastic things around my wrists and put me in his van. He did up my seat belt real tight and told me not to move. I didn't have my booster seat, so couldn't see out the window.'

Grady explained that the man had driven into a garage, closed the door and helped Grady out of the van. When the counsellor asked more questions, Grady described the home. There were two bedrooms, a living room, a kitchen and two bathrooms. He said the man took off the plastic things on his wrists and put him into a room that had a bathroom as part of it. The man locked the bedroom door. The bedroom had a television set and the man said he could watch television if he wanted to. Later, Grady said the man went out and came back with pizza. He gave Grady a couple of pieces of pizza and a milkshake. Grady said he told him that he wasn't supposed to eat pizza or have milk, but the man made him eat it anyway. He explained rather sheepishly that he'd had diarrhoea all the next day. The man must have realised that Grady had been telling the truth and asked him what he could eat.

'I can have soup,' Grady had suggested.

When asked whether the man had hurt him, Grady related that the man had hit him on the face when he balked at eating the pizza and milkshake, so he knew he had better not argue with him. Careful probing and questions confirmed what the physical examination had shown - that he had not been sexually abused. Grady did say something that was interesting, 'The man said he only liked little girls. He said he didn't like little boys.'

So, Grady was saved the shame of being sexually abused because the man only abused little girls.

'Then why did he kidnap Grady?' Denise asked.

'Who knows? Do you think it could be something personal – possibly against you or Blaine?' Dan asked.

Denise and Blaine looked at each other then shrugged their shoulders. 'Because I'm a police officer, I'm wondering if it could be someone I've arrested, and they have a grudge against me,' she said pensively.

'That could be the case. Why don't you look through the cases you've been involved in recently and see if anybody surfaces that might have a grudge and do such a thing,' he suggested.

'I'll do that. Now, can we take our son home?' she asked as she looked from Dan, to the doctor and the counsellor.

'We're done here. This has been one of the 'good' ones. I'm so glad he hasn't been sexually abused. However, he was kidnapped so he might need counselling,' added the child psychologist.

'I'll keep an eye on him and the first sign of trouble I'll call you,' Denise promised.

When they got Grady home, the first thing Denise did was give him a bath. By this time, it was dinner time, and it was good to have the four of them back together for the meal. Grady was exhausted and went to bed right after dinner and slept through the night. Denise, Blaine and even Kali kept checking on him to make sure he was having a good night.

At work the next day, Denise went over her case files and one name kept coming forward, that of 'Uncle Walter.' She had a picture of him on file and gave it to Dan to show to Grady.

'I'll bring several pictures to show him and 'Uncle Walter' will be in the group,' he promised.

That evening Dan and another officer went to Denise's home and when he had Grady settled at their dining room table, he said, 'Grady, I need your help with something.'

Grady looked up at him nodding his head.

'I am going to show you some pictures of people. I want you to look at them and tell me if you know any of them,' Dan said gently.

He put all the photographs in front of Grady and watched as the child carefully examined each one. Then his eyes got wide

13

and he pointed excitedly at one of the photographs. He thumped the picture with his index finger and said, 'That's the man with the puppy. He's the one who made me stay in the bedroom and eat bad things.'

'Thank you, Grady. You've really been a help to us,' he said as he ruffled his lovely red curls.

Grady smiled and looked over at his mother who had tears in her eyes. 'What's the matter Mom? Did I do something wrong?'

She realised that Grady misunderstood her expression. She was overwhelmed with guilt knowing that in a small way she was responsible for his abduction. She reached over and slid him onto her lap. 'No, sweetheart – you've done well. I'm very proud of you.'

It was with great pleasure that Dan and another officer were able to arrest 'Uncle Walter' and charge him with an even more serious offence – that of kidnapping. He admitted that he'd taken Grady to get back at Denise because she'd been the arresting officer.

Denise was pleased to know that he would be in jail for several years and had the pleasure of telling the little girl's mother that her brother, Walter had been charged with another more serious offence and would not be a threat to her daughter in the future.

Chapter 3

Dan's brother, Steve Jeffries phoned Dan one September day and asked if he could come up to Edmonton from Calgary to discuss an important issue. Dan asked him whether he wanted Becky to be there when he talked to him. 'I don't care if she's there – she might be able to give some advice as well.'

When Steve arrived, and they were settled at the kitchen table with cups of coffee, Steve began, 'As you know, I've been in Human Resources with a Calgary oil company for years, but I'm seriously thinking about immigrating to Australia. We visited my Aunt Deanna there a couple of years ago and both Arlene and I loved it there. Now that our kids are grown up and married, I've been offered a wonderful opportunity.'

'Tell me about it,' prompted Dan.

'I've been headhunted over the internet from a financial company that started up about a year ago. They're quite large with almost four hundred employees. They need someone with my experience to set up and run their Human Resources Department. The position I would hold would be as Head of Human Resources. I would have three areas reporting to me; Human Resources itself; Training and Development and Payroll. They have offered me a wonderful employment contract that will last for one year.'

'Will you have to get a work permit to work there?' Becky asked.

'Yes, I will, but the company will take care of that. They've been recruiting in Australia for over a year but haven't been able to find anyone with my experience, so they said they can fast-track the work permit,' he added. The others could see how excited he was about this new idea.

'Will Arlene go with you?' Dan asked.

'Yes, she will, but I don't think she'll be able to work there. Financially we won't need her to work because of my huge salary, so that's no problem. The company will provide a furnished apartment which is part of the deal and they will even supply a leased company car.'

'I can see why you're excited about this! I would be too. You're going to accept it aren't you?' Dan teased.

'I sure am tempted, but I wanted your advice before I signed on the dotted line,' Steve added.

'When would you start?' Becky asked.

'In a month! So, we don't have much time to get our affairs in order at this end,' Steve agreed. 'We'll put our home with an agent to rent it for the year and will store most of our belongings. I think I'll even sell my car and buy a new one when I get back.'

'I think I'd be interested in buying that from you,' suggested Dan. 'With us expecting a baby in April we'll need a bigger vehicle.'

'That would be great and would be one less problem for us to deal with,' said Steve with a sigh.

So, it was all arranged, and within the month Steve and Arlene were off to Sydney Australia to begin their new adventure. They were both jet-lagged when they arrived on the Saturday morning in late October and had two days to settle in before Steve started work on the Monday. They both hoped that they would be able to make a trip to the Gold Coast of Queensland to see Steve's Aunt Deanna some time soon.

Steve had not met the CEO of his new company, Andy Waddell in person. They had only met via SKYPE on a conference call that included their CFO, Edward Upfield. At their first face-to-face meeting in the company's conference room, they shook hands. Steve noted that Andy Waddell was in his early forties. He was a good-looking man, tall, with an athletic look about him. Edward Upfield was a more severe man, also tall and athletic, but noted that he didn't look too friendly. It was clear that he would be called Edward – not Ed. They discussed the position and had Steve complete all the documents required for the lease of the apartment and car and to set up a Superannuation retirement fund etc. The paperwork seemed endless.

Then Andy took him to his work station. Steve was surprised to see that all the offices were open-area – even Andy's station had others seated around him. If any of the managers or executives wanted privacy, there were several meeting rooms in each section. Steve's area had six employees - three managers and four support staff. Steve was introduced to the Human Resources Manager, Bianca Arnold. He guessed her age to be in her early forties. When he met her, he wondered if she'd applied for his position and made a note to himself to ask Andy why she had not been promoted. She was very friendly and promised him that she would help him settle into his new position.

Andy then introduced him to the Training Manager, Charlotte Sterling and her male assistant Bill Andrews. He guessed that Charlotte was in her mid-thirties. She was very well dressed and groomed. They shook hands but soon Charlotte had to rush off to the training room to oversee a training program.

The third manager was the Payroll Manager, Carrie Fellows. This woman appeared to be rushed off her feet but had a friendly smile on her rather chubby face. Steven admitted to her that he was not an expert in payroll, so he would be counting on her to keep him informed of any developments or problems.

The next few days were spent figuring out what was required of him. The major issue was that the Human Resources Policies and Procedures of the company were from the dark ages and had to be revised and accepted by a licensing board within six months. Steve knew this alone would be a monumental task and that evening when he went home to Arlene, he warned her that he would likely be putting in a tremendous amount of overtime.

'I knew that would be the case, so I'll keep myself busy doing other things. Just getting to know Sydney and Australia will keep me out of mischief. I think I'll join some of the women's clubs your Aunt Deanna told me about. She suggested that I investigate the local Probus and View Clubs and possibly join a Rotary Club. We'll both be so busy, I won't balk at you having to work overtime,' she assured him. 'We'll both do our own thing and not be offended if the other one's busy. It looks as if your biggest crunch will last for about six months. Maybe it will ease off after that,' she concluded.

They decided that they should buy a little car for Arlene to use to get to the meetings and to explore the Sydney sites. Steve wished he could join her but found out everything she'd learned about Sydney when they talked during dinner about what had happened during their days. Most nights, Steve would go into the second bedroom that he'd set up as an office and continued working till about nine o'clock. They would watch the ten o'clock news and go to bed. In the mornings Steve made it clear that he didn't expect her to get up when he did. Instead, he would pick up some breakfast at a cafeteria in his office building.

On the Thursday of his first week, Steve asked the Human Resources Manager, Bianca Arnold to join him in one of the meeting rooms. 'Thanks for coming,' he started, 'I need your input to tell me all about your responsibilities as Human Resources Manager and any areas where you're having problems.'

They discussed Human Resources issues and he was surprised when he read her job description. It was only one paragraph long and didn't identify what she did.

He went to his work station and printed out a sheet, then returned to the meeting room. 'Here's a copy of the information that should be on a job description. You'll notice that it too has a single paragraph like your existing one to briefly tell what the job is all about. However, what's missing is what are called key performance indicators or KPIs. These headings list the important functions of your job.'

Bianca looked questioningly at him and asked, 'Can you give me what you think would be one of my KPIs?'

'Sure. One of your responsibilities would be recruiting and filling vacancies in the company. Another would be to ensure that all job descriptions were up to date. A third would be to monitor the performance appraisal system. Do you see what I mean?'

'Yes, I do, and I think I won't have any problem choosing the KPIs for my job.'

'Well, it doesn't end there,' he cautioned and saw her eyebrows raise in a questioning way.

'For instance, under the KPI relating to recruiting you would identify the tasks you would do to complete that function. You would do the same for each of your KPIs.'

She nodded her head and added, 'I wonder why they don't have that kind of information on the job descriptions here? I've enrolled in evening classes to obtain a Human Resources Diploma, but we haven't got to job descriptions or performance appraisals yet.'

'Why don't you take a stab at writing up your KPIs and list the tasks you do to complete them? After you've done that, I'll help you set standards of performance, so you'll know you've done what you were supposed to do.'

'Can you give me an example of a standard of performance?' she asked.

'A standard of performance is a kind of yardstick against which performance in a particular part of a job is measured. It's usually a series of brief statements about the quality and quantity expected within specific time frames. Let's say one of your tasks is to hire three sales personnel. The standard of performance would read: 'Hire three sales personnel who have a minimum of three years' directly related experience by May 1, 20___, at a salary range of $40,000 to $45,000 per annum.'

'Standards of performance have three or four criteria: quality, quantity, time and sometimes cost. For example: Quality: - 3 years' directly related experience; Quantity: - 3 sales personnel; Time: - By May 1, 20___. Cost: - Salary range of $40,000 to 45,000 per annum. Does that make sense?' he asked.

'Yes, and I can see that my work will be cut out for me to update all the job descriptions in the company. I'll start with mine and will give it to you to evaluate when I'm finished,' she said as she smiled at him.

At the end of the meeting he said, 'I'm going to be so busy putting together the policies and procedures that it will be difficult for me to stay on top of HR issues. I'd like you to keep track of anything that happens in your area during the week and put it in a report to give to me every Friday afternoon. If anything, important needs my attention, please know that I can be interrupted at any time.'

She nodded and agreed to do the report. Steve had learned from Andy that she'd come up the corporate ladder through the clerical path to her position and had started taking courses at the university to expand her knowledge of Human Resources. Steve encouraged Bianca to continue her studies and added that if she had any questions about her studies, to feel free to ask him about them. Steve felt very comfortable after this interview and knew she would co-operate with him.

The next day, he arranged to meet with Charlotte Sterling. He learned that she'd been in the position for a year, but although she was Training Manager, she did not do any of the training herself. He detected an atmosphere of hostility in her when he started the interview. As he had with the Human Resources Manager, he examined her job description and saw that it was also a short paragraph that didn't really tell him what she did. He explained about KPIs and standards of performance and asked her to update her job description accordingly.

She grudgingly agreed to do so.

At the end of the interview, he repeated what he had said to the HR manager, 'I'm going to be so busy putting together the HR policies and procedures that it will be difficult for me to stay on top of training issues. I'd like you to keep track of anything that happens in your area and put it in a report to give to me every Friday afternoon. If anything, important needs my attention please know that I can be interrupted at any time.'

He then gave her a form for her to complete. The form related to the training that had been completed within the past year. The columns in the report asked who had requested the training; who had gone to the training; why they had been sent to the training, and what was the result of the training.

'I can't do that,' she said with a huff. 'I don't have that kind of information available to me.'

'Why not? You're in charge of training – surely you've kept records of that information.'

'Well things aren't very formal here.'

'That training information should be on the employee's personnel files. Could you please liaise with the Bianca and obtain that information?'

Reluctantly she agreed, but he could see that she didn't like the idea that she had to account for what she'd been doing or more likely not been doing over the past year.

Later that afternoon, Andy called Steve into his office. 'How has your first week gone?'

Steve explained about the two meetings he'd had so far and said he would be talking with Carrie Fellows the Payroll Manager the next Monday.

'How did those meetings go?' the CEO asked.

'The one with Bianca went fine and she seems very co-operative. I'll be asking all three of my reports to update their job descriptions and send me information every Friday afternoon relating to what's going on in their departments. I've spoken with Bianca and Charlotte about this and will be doing the same with Carrie on Monday. However, I think I've found a problem in the Training Department.'

When he said this, Andy looked at him in surprise. 'What kind of problem?'

Steve explained the conversation he'd had with Charlotte that day, showed him a copy of the form he'd asked her to complete and asked Andy what he thought about the fact that there were no records of training conducted in the past year.'

'There should be. We have forms we send out to supervisors and managers to be filled in about training, and I know that the performance appraisals have something about training on them. I'm sure she can come up with the information you need. If you run into any difficulties, let me know.'

He continued, 'I've rounded up all the Human Resources Policies and Procedures that are presently in place. As you go through and revise them, please send them to me and we can discuss the contents.'

'I'll do that.' Steve promised.

Steve spent the weekend going through the mishmash of policies and procedures Andy had given to him and began making derogatory remarks under his breath.

'What are you muttering about?' Arlene asked.

'These policies and procedures have to be thrown out completely. I'm going to have to start from scratch. It's good I have lots of research material with me, so I can do that. But it will be a lot of work, because everything will have to relate to Australian, not Canadian laws. I'll have to do a lot of research to find those differences,' he said shaking his head. The task was going to be even more complicated than he'd originally thought and would take much more effort on his part.

'I can see you have your work cut out for you,' she agreed.

He took a break and asked, 'Have you looked into joining any of those groups?'

'Yes, I spoke with a nearby group who meet for Probus every month. I'll be going to my first meeting with them this Wednesday and they have a bus trip planned for the week after that.'

'Good. That will keep you out of mischief,' he said as he sipped the cup of coffee, she'd just given him.

The next week Steve spoke to Carrie Fellows and found her to be very cooperative. She also agreed to work on updating her job description and would send weekly reports on the Friday afternoons. By four-thirty that Friday afternoon, Steve had received e-mails from both Carrie and Bianca enclosing their reports but there was still nothing from Charlotte. He was just about to go to her office when Andy phoned and asked him to come to his office. He didn't sound very happy.

When Steve had settled into a chair, Andy blurted out, 'Charlotte has just handed in her resignation.'

'Why?' Steve asked, rather shocked at the announcement.

'She says she can't work with you.' Andy stated. 'That you expect too much from her.'

'She has refused to submit the reports I asked for last week and as far as I know, she hasn't updated her job description. I haven't talked to her directly since last Friday. I thought I would give her time to do what she needed to do to give me the information I asked for. I learned today that she hasn't even talked with Bianca to see the personnel records, so she can determine what training has been done. Bianca says there has been nothing added to the personnel files relating to training done by the employees in the past year, so we'll have to chase down that information the hard way.' Steve replied. He was fed up with Charlotte's attitude and was secretly glad she'd given her resignation.

'I was afraid that was happening. I should have been on top of things more. I guess we'll have to start recruiting for a replacement.' Andy concluded, giving Steve permission to replace the unacceptable employee.

'In the meantime, I'll see if Bill Andrews her clerk can find any records for us.' said Steve.

Steve spent that weekend writing a job description for a replacement Training Manager. Andy had shown him the reports that were already in place relating to training that he could adapt to the new description. He also knew there were some policies and procedures in place in the old system. By Monday, he'd completed a description for what he thought a training manager should be doing in a company. He gave that job description to Bianca and asked her to advertise and set up a short list of people he would interview for the position.

'What is the salary range for that position?' he asked Bianca.

She replied, 'We don't really have salary ranges. We just offer a salary and sometimes negotiate it, but we don't really have salary ranges for positions.'

He was flabbergasted. This was really an antiquated company he decided. 'I can see there's another thing that eventually you and I will have to work on.'

The job proved to be very gruelling, especially seeing Steve had to now find another Training Manager. Bianca set up several interviews for those on the short-list. Over thirty people had applied for the position, but she had chosen four who had the qualifications Steve had asked for.

Steve felt that the third applicant, Eddie Bradshaw was a winner, and felt that he had the ideal candidate. Eddie had lots of training experience and seemed to be on the same wavelength as Steve regarding the importance of effective employee training. Eddie was also an accomplished trainer himself, so could do some of the in-house training, which would save their company a considerable amount of money. Eddie was satisfied with the salary he was offered. Steve explained that he'd been hired in mid-range for the position and explained that when he would have his three-month evaluation, he would qualify for a raise in salary depending on how well he did the job.

'I'll need you to work with your assistant Bill Andrews to obtain the information I need about last year's training. You might have to speak to the heads of each department to obtain that information. Let me know if you run into any problems with that,' Steve instructed.

Steve struggled along day after day and Arlene started getting worried because he was so stressed by the end of a week.

'I don't like what I see,' she said one evening. 'You're so stressed out. Is there anything I can do to help?'

'You can massage my shoulders every night – they're so tight they're giving me a headache,' he complained.

'I think there might be a solution. Leave it with me and I'll try to fix things.'

The next evening Arlene announced that she'd arranged for Steve to have a Shiatsu massage every Saturday morning in their home. The masseuse was a woman whose regular job was teaching elementary students. She explained that her wrists weren't strong enough to do it full-time, but she had some regular clients she saw during the week. Steve did seem much more relaxed after his massages and they both felt it was worth the expense.

The massages seemed to help him through his week, but the pressures at work got worse. One weekend, Steve sent the following long and rambling e-mail to his brother Dan:

Dear Dan,

I need to talk to you about what's been happening at work. It's turning into a nightmare.

Although the company advocates a work/life balance, the six-month deadline for upgrading the policies and procedures manuals has been an almost impossible task. For the first four months of my employment, I have not taken a day off except around Christmas. I've worked weekends and often bring work home in the evenings. At first, I thought it was worth it because both Andy and the government licensing authority are slowly but surely approving the policies and procedures I've prepared and I'm meeting the tight deadlines.

Dan responded with sympathy and support and asked to be kept informed. The next e-mail came a month later:

Things have gone from bad to worse. This month (five and a half months after I was hired) the company obtained approval from the governing body for their license. I thought I could relax but find that there are things going on that I deeply disapprove of.

Under the surface, there are many problems. In many areas, Andy sabotages my achievements and does not give me the autonomy that was promised in my offer letter. Many of Andy's stalling tactics reflect upon the smooth-running of the HR department and make me appear incompetent. Andy excludes me from the decision-making process and does not allow me to run the HR department the way I think it should be run. The new policies and procedures can't be implemented until all our supervisors obtain training on how to use them. When I scheduled training sessions for them, Andy cancelled the training with no explanation. I would be doing the training myself because the new training manager is not an expert in job description writing and doesn't know how to properly conduct performance appraisals.

*Shortly after the HR Policies and Procedures were approved, they were put on the company intranet, so managers and employees would have access to them. However, Andy made comments to me several times, that he did not believe that the job descriptions needed upgrading. They're in terrible shape with just a paragraph that describes what people do. He will not allow me to upgrade the position descriptions nor provide training to the managers on how to do so for their staff. This went against the policies and procedures approved by the government body. By law, we're supposed to implement **all** the policies and procedures.*

I also became aware of the high incidence of nepotism in this company. Not only are family members working in the same departments, but most of the executive I've learned are Andy's personal friends.

Just before the licence was granted, Andy began making comments to me about reverting to the original performance appraisal system when they would come due in September. This too will contravene the government licensing. It was at this time that I became aware that the initial stage of performance appraisals that identified the objectives for each employee (that should have been completed in July of last year before I started with the company) had not been done. I reminded Andy of this and he decided to complete the initial part of the performance appraisals in March - only three months before the employees would be evaluated on their performance for the entire previous year. Even at this late date - instead of using the government approved performance appraisal system, Andy decided to use the company's old ineffective score card system. This contravened what had been agreed upon when the company obtained their government licence.

He leaves me out of the loop, makes crucial HR decisions without my input or knowledge. For instance, Andy makes employees redundant instead of going through the properly documented disciplinary process. One employee disagreed with him once too often and the next day the announcement was made that his position was being made redundant. I learned after-the-fact that he'd made the man's position redundant - with no consultation with me before doing so. As head of human resources, I should have been consulted before action was taken.

Andy explained that anyone who did not follow the company vision would have to go. I've interpreted this to be that if employees didn't follow Andy's way of doing things, they would be asked to leave.

Sorry to dump this all on you, but just had to let you know how unhappy I am working for this CEO.

Love, Steve

In a later e-mail Steve said:

This nightmare is still going on...

Andy uses bullying tactics with his direct reports (the executive of the company – including me). Those meetings have become a matter of him taking strips off the executive members. I've cautioned Andy that this was something that just wasn't done in public. Andy agreed that it wasn't right - but continues to do so.

Upon monitoring the absenteeism of employees, I noted that several departments had extremely high levels of sick leave. I now realize that it was likely because of the level of abuse they are subjected to by their supervisors, managers and executives who use Andy's behaviour as a benchmark for acceptable corporate (bullying) behaviour.

Much of Andy's harassment involves other executive members. Bill Carmichael, the head of Group Risk, was instrumental in the company obtaining its licence because he insisted that Andy follow the compliance requirements. Andy objected to many of his suggestions and resisted vigorously. Three days after the company received its licence, Bill was given a redundancy package (without my knowledge of course). Andy's unofficial reason for this redundancy was that Bill had been making advances on female employees and that Bill had come into work under the influence of alcohol. (I think Bill could sue him for defamation of character.) Because I was not consulted before this was done, I seriously question that these accusations were true.

The next day, Bill came to the Human Resources Department to sign some papers, and I took him aside to ask him what had happened. Bill explained that he had received no warning about his demise - was just told that his position had been made redundant and to clear out his belongings. During this conversation, Bill warned me that my own position was probably next and described the signs I should watch for. The first sign of trouble would be if Andy started taking some of my responsibilities away from me, and the second would be that he would start degrading me in public.

It didn't take long to happen. That same afternoon, Andy told me that he would be moving the payroll function into the finance department (I have no objection to that – it probably should have been under their umbrella anyway).

Then, one week later, he came to my open-area office to have me sign off on several new Human Resources Policies and Procedures. I was startled to see that Andy wanted the company to return to using its old antiquated job description and performance appraisal systems that were contrary to those accepted when the company obtained its licence. I tried to make Andy see that the old system simply didn't work, but he wouldn't listen to me and tried to force me to sign off on the new system. Andy kept relating to how much he had given in relating to the new system and that I should be willing to bend as well.

I knew that if I agreed to the changes, it would go completely against the government licensing regulations. I told Andy I couldn't approve of the revised policy but suggested that he do so instead. I didn't want to become the "fall guy" which could happen if I signed the documents and the governing body questioned the changes.

It was then that Andy completely lost it. His face was beet red and he became so frustrated at my refusal that he publicly humiliated me by shouting so loudly that my entire staff and others nearby heard what he said. I contemplated taking Andy into a nearby private office but decided not to when I smelled alcohol on his breath. Shortly after his outburst, Andy left my work station and spoke to Bianca Arnold, the Human Resources Manager (who sits behind my station).

As I was leaving the office that afternoon, my staff was still working. Two of my staff asked me if I was okay. They explained that the whole floor had heard Andy yelling at me. They were very upset at how Andy had treated me and said they could clearly hear the confrontational aspects of the session. They also mentioned that others who were not working in the Human Resources department had overheard Andy's angry words. The new Training Manager stated that he thought it was a case of harassment - that the CEO was out of control. I later learned that Eddie Bradshaw, the new Training Manager had not heard the confrontation, but was just concerned when the other two employees discussed the situation with him. The next morning, Bianca confirmed that she too had smelled alcohol on Andy's breath.

I have decided to send a letter to the Board of Directors charging Andy with workplace bullying and harassment. I can't take any more of this shit.

Wish me luck, Steve

Another follow-up e-mail:

The past week has been another traumatic one for me. I submitted my letter accusing Andy of workplace bullying and harassment and had an interview with the Chairman of the Board. He said he would investigate the situation and would get back to me in about a week.

In the meantime, at an executive meeting the next day, Andy asked two of his executives to work with me to finalise the company performance appraisal plan. Of course, I objected because neither of the executives had any background in human resources. The next Monday the three of us met, and I was amazed when the CFO Edward Upfield (who is a very close friend of the CEO) took over the meeting. He explained how he felt the process should work and outlined his beliefs on a whiteboard. The other executive agreed with his information. I sat amazed, because they had fully endorsed the system that had received government approval! I told them this and we agreed to meet in two days to finalise the policy (which would be identical to that already in place with the licensing body). I was elated.

When we met two days later, Edward Upfield did a one hundred and eighty-degree turn-around (he must have discussed it with Andy). The other executive member nodded his assent to using their old method. I glared at them both as I stated, 'He got to you, didn't he?' and disgustedly walked out of the meeting.

Every time I see Andy, I seethe inside at the way I've been treated. I realize that as Head of Human Resources, if I condone such bullying behaviour, the rest of the staff will not have protection from bullying and feel I must set an example. Normally I would be the one investigating such claims as is shown by the new company policy; however, the chairman of the board has said that it will be investigated by a former police officer who works in the Risk Department of our company.

I contacted a lawyer to see whether I can charge the company with breach of contract because I was not being allowed to do the job I'd been hired to do. I also investigated how I can act to fight the bullying I've received from my superior.

I will keep you informed.

Love, Steve

Dan had many talks with Steve on SKYPE. He was devastated to learn that Steve had investigated the bullying and harassment issue and learned that Australia has no laws that protect employees against such issues.

Dan said, 'The Occupational Health and Safety Act in Canada covers that issue. Have you investigated that Act?'

'Yes, I have. I've done a word check on all six States and the Federal Occupational Health and Safety Acts and nowhere in those documents could I find the words, workplace bullying, harassment or violence. My lawyer doesn't seem to feel I have a chance at winning my case. She's told me that it can take up to five years to get to court (which is my only option) and can cost about $100,000. So, tomorrow I'm going to tell the chairman of the board that I'm taking a leave of absence until the issue is dealt with. So, I'll be at home for a while and hope they get their act together and discipline Andy. If I don't hear from the chairman of the board within two weeks, I'll tell Andy to stuff his job and hand him my resignation.

Two weeks later came this e-mail:

Well, it's over. After spending only six months with the company, I handed in my resignation to the chairman of the board with a letter explaining all the things Andy was doing to undermine my authority. I included a veiled threat that I might charge them with wrongful dismissal because they literally forced me to leave. Bill was right when he warned me that I would be next. Well Andy's succeeded in getting rid of me. You can imagine how upset I am.

Dan phoned right away. 'Will you be staying in Australia?' he asked.

'Arlene and I will be coming home in about a month. We'll have to give up the apartment in two weeks, so we will go to the Gold Coast to visit Aunt Deanna until we fly home. We can't stay in Australia because my work permit is now null and void. I just wish I could smash the bastard!'

'So do I. I'm so sorry this has happened to you,' lamented Dan.

Two days later the following e-mail arrived from Steve:

My lawyer has been able to get me three month's severance pay, so at least that's a bonus, but she has warned me that I will likely not receive a good reference from the company, so I hope that doesn't affect my chances of finding work again in Canada. I still can't believe how far behind Australia is in their employment laws. Most companies here don't have proper job descriptions and their performance appraisal systems are terrible and not fair to the employees.

On a more pleasant note, we'll be off to the Gold Coast soon and we have sold Arlene's car. It will be warmer there and I must tell you I need all the warmth I can get before coming back to the Canada even though it will be the beginning of spring when we get home.

Love, Steve

Steve and Arlene were met at the Coolangatta Airport and immediately recognized their Aunt Deanna. She was almost identical to Steve's mother Dorothea. They'd corresponded via e-mail and she'd been informed about the awful time Steve had been through so went out of her way to make their visit a good one. She had a two-bedroom apartment and soon had them settled in their room.

They had the meal she'd prepared, and they told her again the step-by-step incidents that had led to him leaving his job. 'I'm so sorry that happened,' she commiserated. 'Do you feel up to having some adventures while you're here? Or are you too tired for that?' she asked.

'No. We'd love to see more of Australia. What do you have in mind?'

'Well, we could get tickets to the three main theme parks - Sea World, Wet 'N Wild, and Dream World. Or we could go to the Australia Zoo.'

'Is that the one that Steve Irwin owned?' Arlene asked.

'Yes. His wife and two children Bindi and Robert are now managing it.'

'I'd like to go to that one,' Steve agreed.

'Another choice you have is one I'd like to take. We could drive up to the Whitsundays and take a sailing catamaran to Hamilton Island. I know you're a SCUBA diver Steve and you can't come to Australia without diving here. Arlene and I can snorkel while you're diving. What do you think?' she said as she looked from one to the other.

Steve and Arlene looked at each other and both nodded their heads.

'I think we should see when that can be arranged.' Steve stated.

Deanna added another choice, 'I know it will take us a while to drive up to the Whitsundays, however we could take a plane instead. The airlines are having a price war, so we could get some cheap seats. Which way would you prefer?'

'Well, because we really don't have too much time here, maybe we should fly,' said Steve looking to Arlene for approval. She nodded her head.

'I can look into the airfares and book us into a hotel for the night before and after we sail,' she suggested.

The four events were arranged, and everyone had a wonderful time at all of them. Steve and Arlene also spent several afternoons enjoying the sun on Burleigh Beach, and enjoyed having leisurely meals at the Burleigh Heads Surf Club restaurant, that had lovely views of the surfers riding the waves.

'I'm going to miss this,' admitted Steve.

'We'll have to come back again and hopefully we'll enjoy it better than we have this time,' said Arlene and then looked guiltily at Deanna. 'I didn't mean this part of our trip,' she was quick to add.

Steve and Arlene were much more relaxed when they returned to Calgary. Because they'd signed a one-year lease for people to rent their home, their next chore was to find a place to rent in the interim and get their furniture out of storage. In the meantime, they stayed with their mother Dorothea who drove them around to car dealerships and real estate rental offices. He sent another e-mail to Dan:

Hi Dan,

We got home last week and are staying with Mom. She's been great, driving us around to car dealerships. I'll be picking up my new car next week. This week we also found a lovely two-bedroom home that's a few blocks away from Mom's and will move in a week from now. I just hope all our furniture will fit into it. I know we'll have to leave one of the queen-sized beds and the dresser that goes with it in storage, but hopefully the rest of our stuff will fit.

As soon as we're settled, we'd like you to come down for a visit. Let me know when that can be arranged, possibly two or three weeks from now. As soon as the lease on our own home is up, we 'll be moving back there.

It's good to be home and after a wonderful time with Deanna on the Gold Coast, both of us are very relaxed. My next chore is for Arlene and me to find jobs. Thankfully, I earned so much on the job that I can afford to wait for the right job to come along.

We look forward to seeing you in about a month.

Love, Steve.

Dan wrote back:

My family would never fit into your two-bedroom home. Why don't you come up to Edmonton? We've got room here for the two of you.

Have you looked at any jobs in Edmonton? I saw an advertisement in the newspaper that the government is looking for Human Resources specialists. I've enclosed a file with the advertisement. I know you like Calgary, but if you can't find a job there, would you consider moving here?

Love, Dan

Steve wrote back:

Thanks for sending the advertisement. I e-mailed my CV and they called me today and want me to come up for an interview. They have a senior position available, so it's worth looking into. Can I stay at your place for a night or two?

I also need your advice on what I should tell them about my last job.

Love, Steve

Dan phoned him and said, 'Steve, of course you can stay here. Why don't you bring Arlene with you?'

'She's got to be here to start unpacking the boxes,' Steve explained.

'Well, if you get the job here, should she really be doing that?' Dan questioned.

'You've got a point. Maybe we should stop unpacking and both of us come up tomorrow for the interview.'

'You know you're always welcome here, and Becky will be home when you arrive. Now about your second question about what you should tell them about your last job. I think you must be honest with them. I think you should write down all the things that went wrong and why you left the company. If you don't, they'll wonder what you've been doing for the past

eight or nine months since you left your last Canadian job.'
Dan recommended.

Steve decided to do exactly that, and the three people on the
panel seemed very sympathetic as he described the horrific
situation he'd been placed in. He admitted, 'I've been told by
my lawyer that they will likely not give a good reference, so
you'll have to take my word that what I've told you is the
truth.'

He left the interview wondering what the verdict would be. He
and Arlene were back in Calgary two days later when he
received a call from the head of recruitment telling him that he
had the job and they wanted him to start in two weeks time.
They'd contacted his former Canadian references and they'd
given glowing reports about how competent he was. They also
admitted that they'd phoned the Australian company, but
Bianca had refused to give a reference (as she had been
instructed to do). The head of the government recruitment was
very qualified and knew that in most cases that kind of refusal
would mean that they had fired the employee. He also knew
that Bianca used to report to Steve, so he asked the questions
that needed to be asked and she finally admitted that Steve had
given his notice after he had been bullied by the CEO.

Steve and Arlene faced several problems. They'd just signed a
lease to rent a home for four months, and they still owned a
home that would still be rented for four months.

'What should we do?' Arlene asked Steve. She wanted him to
accept the position.

'I think the first thing I'll do, is see if we can get out of the
lease on this place. We would only have about three months
left on the lease.'

'Let's try,' suggested Arlene as she located the phone number
of the lease agency. They were both pleased that they would
let them out of their lease. Rental homes were snapped up

quickly because Calgary business was booming, and houses rented very easily.

So, their next step was to arrange for a moving company to move their things to Edmonton. In the meantime, they would go back to Edmonton to find another place to rent and eventually buy a place. Dan again offered his home for them to stay in while they looked for a place.

Steve was excited when he and Arlene arrived home from viewing a home the real estate firm had shown them. The owners said it was vacant right now and they could move in whenever they wanted to. But the thing that they were so excited about was that the owner had been thinking of selling the home and would let them buy it as soon as their home in Calgary was sold.

Everything fell into place, and they were able to sell their home in Calgary just after the lease was up for their tenants. Dan was pleased that their new home was only ten blocks or so from their place. The only drawback was that their mother Dorothea was now living alone in Calgary. Her two sons lived in Edmonton and her daughter Patsy and her family lived in Red Deer that was half way between those two cities.

Arlene obtained a job as an accountant with a small accounting firm that was several blocks from their home. Steve needed their car to get to his job, so Arlene was glad she could walk to work.

They were both thankful that their terrible experience in Australia was over. They loved Australia itself, just didn't like the bullying atmosphere that seemed to permeate most companies.

Chapter 4

While they were visiting their Aunt Deanna in Australia, she'd admitted shyly that she'd met a man she was very fond of. 'His name is Martin Williams and we've decided to move in together in a few months.'

'How did you meet him?' Arlene asked.

Deanna looked down in embarrassment, 'I met him on-line on a dating site.'

'Are you sure he's what he says he is? I understand there are quite a few dating scams out there.' Steve warned.

'Well, first we corresponded via e-mails, then by phone. He's very articulate and mannerly. I met him several months ago and we've hit it off very well – in fact he's stayed overnight here, and I've visited his home near Brisbane a few times.'

'What's he like?' Arlene asked.

'He's a bit over six feet tall, slim, my age, a widower and very mannerly. He emigrated from England seven years ago with his wife, but she died of cancer a couple of years ago.'

'It sounds as if you really like him,' Steve stated.

'Yes, I do. In fact, that's why we've made plans to move in together. I'll be moving into his home near Brisbane – because he would lose too much money if he sold his home.'

'Why would he lose money?' Steve asked.

'The residents don't own the land. They can't have a mortgage, so they must pay cash for their homes. Most of the homes are worth between four and five hundred thousand dollars in value so that's a lot of cash for anyone to have to pay up-front for a home.'

'Wow, that's expensive!' Steve agreed.

'That's not all. In addition to that, they pay a residency fee per month to the management firm,' she announced in disgust. 'I had no knowledge about how a retirement village operated until I met Martin. I learned that the land under the homes is owned by a management firm who set the rules governed by the Queensland Retirement Village Act. I've been thoroughly disgusted with that Act because it heavily favours the land owners and don't seem to give a hoot about the retired people who've bought the properties on it.'

She continued, 'For instance, if residents found that they didn't like their neighbours, became too ill to live in their home or didn't like the environment of the village, they would have to forfeit up to thirty percent of the value of their property.'

'You've got to be joking!' Steve exclaimed.

'No, and that's not all. They would expect owners to pay fifty percent of the capital gains on their property from the time they bought it until they sold it. He's told me he would lose well over two hundred thousand dollars if he sold his home and we moved into another place.'

'Wow! How is that legal?'

'Although most of the residents take their option to buy to a lawyer, most of these lawyers are not aware of the hold the management firm would have on their everyday lives.'

Steve and Arlene made listening noises and Deanna continued, 'Another one of their rules blows my mind. If an additional person (such as me) is to stay in their unit overnight, the resident must report this to the management firm. Can you imagine having to report to a thirty-something woman that you're going to spend the weekend with your fellow?'

She was almost shouting now, 'And management's reasoning for this is that they need to know who's in the homes in case there's an emergency in the village or for evacuation purposes. However, to show you how stupid this ruling is; the residents do *not* have to tell them when they are *not* home overnight. So, the management would not know the number of people there were in the residence if there *was* emergency. To me, this ruling is very pointless and embarrassing to those couples wanting to be together overnight.'

'How archaic is that!' exclaimed Arlene.

'So, what are you going to do?' Steve asked. 'I somehow can't see you living in a retirement village – you're too vital a person.

'Oh, they're a lively bunch – no grass grows under the feet of the occupants. I've met many of them and they're mainly 'with it' people and most seem very intelligent, so it will be interesting living there. They have fabulous facilities – a heated swimming pool with a ramp for those in wheelchairs, a five-star recreation centre with dance floor, stage for productions and a bar for TGIF nights. They offer lots of activities to keep their people occupied and happy. I think I'll like living there,' she said nodding her head.

'And it's no problem for me to move,' she continued, 'because I'm just renting now,' she said as she watched their reaction.

'Do you really want to do that?' Arlene asked.

'It doesn't appear that there's much choice in the matter,' she said with a shake of her head. 'So, I've agreed to move in with Martin. My lease is up in mid-April, so we don't have much time to make the move.'

'Well, please keep us informed. We want you to be happy.' Steve said.

Later, Steve received this e-mail from Deanna,

'Hi Steve and Arlene,

43

This week we're at the final countdown for my move in with Martin. I've been madly packing, and the movers will be coming on April 20th. Martin says there's some paperwork I must sign that will allow me to live with him, so I'll be going there tomorrow to see the management about it.

The next day, Steve received another e-mail from Deanna,

The young village management woman, Michelle gave me a document to sign. She advised me to discuss it with my lawyer before signing it. As you know, I used to be a legal secretary, and noticed that there are two clauses in the agreement that seem illegal to me. Here's what they say:

OCCUPATION OF UNIT

(ii)   releases the Operator from all liability (whether in contract, tort, by statute or otherwise however) in respect of all claims whatever relating to the use and occupation of the Unit by the Guest and the residing within the Village by the Guest

GUEST TO INDEMNIFY OPERATOR

The Guest releases and indemnifies the Operator and agrees to keep the Operator and its employees, agents and contractors released and at all times indemnified to the fullest extent permitted by law from and against all claims of every description whatever incurred by the Operator or for which the Operator may be or become liable whether in contract, tort, by statute or otherwise however and whether during or after the term of the Licence in respect of or arising from, the use and occupation of the Unit by the Guest and the residing in the Village by the Guest.

*I discussed these clauses with my lawyer today. He agreed. The two clauses stated that the management of the complex were **not** responsible for anything that happened to me while I was on their property. Both my lawyer and I agree that they have a duty of care to ensure that **anyone** coming inside their gates, whether they're residents, guests or tradespeople who*

were in the common area should be protected. So, I've
removed those clauses and Martin and I will have to see her
again.

The next evening the following e-mail arrived,

*I can't believe this. They refused to accept the document as we
have altered it. I refused to sign an illegal document, so we
asked them what our other choices were for me to move in
with him. The other two choices were ludicrous. I could move
in with him for three weeks – move out for a day, then move in
for another three weeks etc. How dense is that!*

*The third option would be for Martin to sell his home and buy
it back at the going rate. In the meantime, he would pay the
thirty percent of the value of his property and the fifty percent
of his capitol gain. He would lose two hundred and twenty
thousand dollars! Then he would have to buy it back and pay
the full price for his home!*

*We couldn't agree on any of those choices and it's just five
days until my moving truck comes to get my things. I have
nowhere to go! Martin and I will be talking about this tonight.
I'll keep you informed.*

Love, Deanna

Steve phoned Deanna and commiserated with her. 'What
goofy laws they have in Australia that village operators can
get away with this kind of rip-off. You'll have to get a lawyer
to fight this, but in the meantime, where are you going to
live?'

'Martin and I have contacted a few rental agencies and I'll be
looking at rental units in the area close to where he lives. Then
we'll contact the organization that helps residents of
retirement villages to see if they can get the management to
listen to reason,' she said.

'This must be so hard on you.' Arlene said.

'Yes, I'm a basket case, but I can't wallow in it because my focus must be on finding another place where I can live.'

The next day, they received the following e-mail,

Martin and I were able to find a two-bedroom home about five minutes from his retirement village and I've signed a six-month lease. I've let the movers know and everything is set for me to move on April 20th. I just hope that the owners of the retirement village realize how asinine their decision is and they'll let me move in with him sooner rather than later. We will be contacting the resident's association and hopefully they can help us.

Deanna kept in touch with them. Steve and Arlene were devastated to learn a few months later that the management would not back down; in fact, they reinforced their stand that Martin would have to sell his unit and buy it back. Here's the information sent to Martin by the village management:

As previously advised, should Ms Clark wish to be considered a resident for the purposes of the Act, then the existing residence contract that you have entered into would need to be terminated and a new residence contract (in your name and Ms Clark's name) would need to be entered into. Of course, this will trigger payment of any exit fees under your current residence contract, the issue of a new Public Information Document to both parties and the payment of a new ingoing contribution.

Deanna added the following to her e-mail:

We've been in constant touch with the representatives of the resident's association, but they don't seem to be able to do anything to help us. So, we've decided to go public with the information and will be appearing on national television next week to tell our story. Wish us luck!

Martin and Deanna were pleased with the television news broadcast. They showed Martins home; Deanna's rental unit;

talked with another couple in his complex who'd only had to pay three thousand dollars for a partner to move in; and spoke with the chairman of the Resident's Association. It was a well-done news exposé that told their story in a very factual and heart rendering way. However, nothing changed. As Deanna's next e-mail stated:

In fact, the management group have made it even more difficult for me to stay for a weekend or two. Some of the residents have begun giving me dirty looks and Martin has heard that the manager has been having tea with some of the residents saying that we were lying about our situation.

Soon Deanna's six-month lease was going to be up for renewal, and she had to decide what to do. Martin explained that he would not move out of the retirement village. The tension between her and Martin deepened and finally after doing everything she could to fight the village management, she gave up her fight. When Deanna's lease was up, she quietly moved back to the Gold Coast and did not see Martin again.

Chapter 5

Deanna had really liked the ambiance of the Retirement Village but would never want to be locked into a resort that had exit and capital gains fees. She had made a trip to the Gold Coast three weeks before her lease was up and talked to several of her friends about where she should live. She was contemplating whether she would buy or rent again. One of her friends, Ruth, lived in a Fifty Plus complex and raved about how much she liked it, so Deanna asked her if she could come and see the complex.

Ruth showed her the site, and it was almost identical to the retirement village except they did not have alarms around the homes that residents could push if they needed medical help. It had three hundred individual homes – most being bungalows, but some were two-storey. The owners bought the homes but did not own the property and had to pay a monthly fee for the maintenance of the complex.

Ruth's complex was gated and had a live-in manager and sales office plus a beauty parlour and coffee shop.

There was a huge recreational hall with a dance floor and stage for entertainment. They had many gathering places where small parties could be held and a large area with tables where they could have special sessions such as Happy Hour, play bingo, play cards or darts, a movie theatre that held about 30 people, three swimming pools, a tennis court, 9 lawn bowling greens and a fully equipped exercise room. They had a kitchen and bar as well that could be used by the residents. The grounds were beautifully kept, and everyone seemed to be very friendly.

Deanna would be able to have a dog and there were quite a few dogs in the complex. She wanted a pet, so, before leaving her rental unit, had gone to a shelter, and had purchased a little dog she named Kelly. He was getting on in years but was a lovely little dog.

So, she stayed an extra day on the Gold Coast and started looking at the various Fifty Plus facilities that were available and decided that the one Ruth had shown her was the nicest of them all. She looked at all the units that were available and chose a bungalow that was available right away. She signed the agreement and arranged to move in on August 15th, 2014.

She settled in and was soon involved in many of the complex's activities. It was easy to make friends there, and she soon felt at home. Having a little dog to walk kept her fit and was a magnet for others to talk to her. She knew she had made the right move and thoroughly enjoyed living there. The only fly in the ointment was that the man who lived next door, literally hated dogs. Deanna was friendly with his wife and they became friends despite his obvious dislike for her dog.

Kelly was a relatively quiet dog but did bark if anyone came to the door or walked by on the street when her front door was open. The man complained several times about his barking, but Deanna knew that with several other dogs living on the street, some of the barking was not his. This was the only thing that curtailed her going out and leaving Kelly alone as much as she would have liked to.

In November of that year, Kelly's health went downhill very quickly. He would yelp then stand looking confused until she comforted him. The vet sadly told her that Kelly had developed doggy dementia and being almost blind became terrified. He recommended that he be put to sleep. Sadly, Deanna complied and missed him terribly.

That Christmas she decided to get another little dog – this time a bit younger one who would live a little longer so went to the Animal Welfare League on the Gold Coast and bought little Cookie. She was eight years old and had been used as a breeding dog and must have been abandoned when she became too old to breed. All dogs are de-sexed at the shelter, so she had just been 'fixed' and had to wear a 'halo' for the first week Deanna had her.

Cookie was a rather quiet dog and only barked when someone came to the door or walked by the home which was normal behaviour for all dogs. However, she was also a little escape artist and had learned that if she went under the house, she could come out the front of the house where there was no fence. Deanna was forced to pay $1,000 to hire a carpenter to close the house in around the back yard so she couldn't escape.

In early February, the manager of the complex came to her door, saw the dog and asked if she was a new dog. Deanna said, 'Yes, I got her two months ago from the Animal Welfare League.'

'Well, we had a complaint that she has been barking especially this past weekend. But that isn't the major problem here – our site agreement states that you can bring a dog into the complex when you move in, but if it dies, you can't replace it. So, you will have to get rid of the dog.'

'What!' she said in astonishment. 'There are lots of dogs here. Why am I being singled out?'

'Look at your site agreement.' He advised. 'I will speak to the owners about her and see whether she can stay or not.'

'Who reported her?'

'I can't reveal that, but it was a neighbour.' He explained.

With that he walked back to his buggy and returned to his office in the recreational centre.,

'Oh, my God! What am I going to do?' Deanna wailed after she had shut the front door.

The first thing she did was dig out her site agreement and sure enough there was a clause hidden near the back of the agreement that said, *'No pet will be replaced in the event of their demise.'*

She talked with the neighbour who lived on the other side of her home and explained what had happened.

'What! Who would do something like that?'

'I think we both know who hates dogs in this neighbourhood. The manager said that Cookie was barking a lot this past weekend, but I have been home, all weekend and she hasn't made a peep. However, your little dog barked quite a bit because she would greet your visitors at the door barking excitedly.'

'I'm so sorry that happened,' she said.

'I didn't reveal to the manager that it wasn't my dog barking – he seemed more focused on the fact that I shouldn't have obtained another dog than he was about the barking. So, no, I didn't say anything about her barking.'

'Does her barking bother you?' she asked.

'Not at all. The only time a dog barking would bother me would be if it kept me awake at night. It's normal for dogs to bark when someone comes to their home. So, don't worry about any barking she does. She's such a cutie and I'd never rat on her.'

'Isn't there anything you can do to keep her?'

'I have to wait to see what the owner of the property says. The manager will be speaking with him and will get back to me. In the meantime, I have to prepare myself to lose almost $1,500 that I have invested in her and will not be able to have another pet as long as I live in this complex.'

'You could always move out and move back with another dog?' she suggested

They both chuckled at this suggestion.

The next day she learned that the owner said her dog had to go, so Deanna returned little Cookie to the Animal Welfare League. She would receive no money back even though she had the dog for less than two months. The next day, a neighbour suggested that she could have obtained a letter from her doctor saying she needed a companion dog. This same neighbour had explained that another resident had a dog when she came into the complex, he died, and she was heartbroken because she could not replace the dog. A month ago, just before Christmas, she committed suicide.

Deanna decided that this problem didn't just affect her – it affected everyone in the complex. With most of the residents being over 65, this clause needed to be taken out of the site agreement. She discussed this problem with the Home Owner's Association president, and he was thoroughly disgusted with what had happened and suggested that Deanna put together a letter to present to the owners. He would present the letter on her behalf.

Deanna decided to do so, and prepared documents that proved that the elderly (especially those living alone) benefitted from having a pet. Those pets provide companionships, keep owners active and socializing with others, sharpen their minds, are mood boosters, owner's heart health and stress improves, the dog protects their owners, gives seniors something to get up for in the morning.

She also learned that federal laws would override the site agreement if a doctor recommended that a senior obtain a companion dog.

The Home Owners Association presented the documents to the manager and he had twenty-one days to reply.

Their first response stated they would not remove the clause, but everyone got together and put together an even more thorough document that described the laws and that a complex was either pet-friendly or was not pet-friendly. Since Deanna's complex allowed some pets and not others, they were breaking the law. They finally agreed to remove that clause.

Deanna decided to wait a while before getting another pet because she had received an e-mail from her sister Dorothea explaining how lonely she felt living in Calgary, now that her sons and their families were living in Edmonton.

Deanna phoned her sister. 'Come on down,' Deanna almost shouted. 'Why don't you give up your rental unit and come and live with me for six months?'

Dorothea replied, 'Let me talk to the kids about this. It would be wonderful to see Australia, and now that I have arthritis, it might be less troublesome down there. I'll get back to you after I've spoken to the kids,' she promised.

She contacted Canada Pension to ensure that her Canadian Pension and Old Age Assistance payments would continue even though she was in Australia and was relieved to find out that those funds would continue to be deposited into her Canadian bank account.

Steve and Dan encouraged her to go and it wasn't long until she was winging her way to Australia. Steve suggested that she fly to Hawaii first to break the trip a little, spend a few days there, then go on to the Gold Coast. That's what she did and because she'd never been to Hawaii before, enjoyed that part of her trip as well.

She decided that because she could only stay in Australia for six months, that when she returned to Canada, she would move to Edmonton to live closer to her children, so put her belongings into storage before leaving Canada.

Chapter 6

As Becky's pregnancy progressed and she left the period where she had morning sickness, she was surprised at how much she was able to accomplish. She was able to edit just about the same number of books she'd edited before she decided to work from her home.

Irma, her housekeeper occasionally made dinner before she left for the evening. Becky had interviewed several women before she decided that Irma was the one who best suited her requirements. Irma had a sense of humour that kept them all laughing, and she was wonderful with little Mike. His care had not been part of her responsibilities, but they found he followed her around and insisted on 'helping' her do the chores. He helped her sort the laundry and she lifted him up, so he could put the next load into the washing machine. When that load was done, he 'helped' her put the clothes into the dryer, and when that load was dry, pulled them all out into the basket so Irma could fold them. His next job was to carefully hold the items and distribute them to the correct bedrooms.

He loved shopping with Irma and was on his best behaviour during their trips because he knew he would have a treat when they got home. This was often an ice cream treat of some sort or a mini chocolate bar.

In the evening, Sandy felt her responsibility was to bathe Mike, read him a story and tuck him in for the night.

Becky was constantly amazed had how stress-free her life was with so much assistance from everyone.

Irma insisted that Becky stop for meals and often brought her a fruit snack and cup of tea in the afternoons. Becky often got so engrossed in the books she was editing that she completely lost track of time.

Becky took time to check on the Crime Stoppers progress in presenting the talks to the high school students. The volunteers were finding that they often had to phone their police advisors to obtain answers to the many questions asked by the students. The volunteer association was pleased that it now had four seniors who were able to do two schools each during the weeks, so the number of schools completed were increasing faster than they thought was possible.

Several times, the students reported seeing the synthetic drugs and gave permission for the volunteers to involve the police in an investigation.

Several months into the school term, Dan asked Becky, 'Is there a possibility that I can attend your next Crime Stoppers meeting?'

'Why?' she asked.

'You'll see when I get there,' he said with a grin on his face.

At the next Crime Stoppers meeting, the chairman introduced Dan and said he wished to speak to the volunteers. Dan reached down into a bag he'd brought to the meeting. In it was a plaque that commended the volunteers for the wonderful job they were doing with their student talks. It was a lovely plaque and very professionally done.

'We'll put this up in our office,' said Mark Handley, as he thanked Dan for recognizing their efforts.

Dan continued, 'Your talks have become even more important as the days go on. The synthetic drug trade has invaded our youth and we're having a terrible time keeping them from hurting our youngsters. Some of the people selling these synthetic drugs are earning up to thirty thousand dollars a day, so it's hard to discourage them from selling them when the profits are so good. There's a new counterculture that exploits the legal loopholes that give users a mind-altering high by changing the chemical makeup of synthetic drugs to keep ahead of what we, the police, can do to stop them. Our government has imposed a blanket ban on possession or selling substances like alcohol, tobacco and food that have substantially the same effect as a dangerous drug. However, stores throughout the province are still openly selling illicit psycho-active drugs which mimic marijuana, cocaine, LSD, and ecstasy. Some of these drugs have up to one hundred times the active ingredient in illicit drugs such as cannabis, making users guinea pigs and crash-test dummies, while the criminals rake in the profits.'

'Sex shop owners and tobacco shops are still the main suppliers, despite new laws banning their sale. Synthetic cannabis is sold as a tea for eighty dollars for a three-gram packet. These special teas are dipped in a potentially fatal hallucinogenic substance that has led directly to the deaths of youngsters. '

'There are now up to two hundred different brands of these drugs. They're called such names as K2, Black Mamba, Smacked, Spice, Minga and N-Bombs. There have been many deaths and the 251-NBOMe seems to be one of the deadliest. Our biggest problem is that we don't know what's in many of them – but we do know the results – organ failure, seizures, and paranoia.'

'Producers of these substances have been traced back to factories in China where they are selling them on the web. They're shipped by courier and seem to be able to slip under the radar of custom officials because of their packaging.'

'So, you're fulfilling an important part in our attempt to warn kids about these lethal drugs. Keep up the good work.'

That evening Dan told Becky about a case he had investigated that day. The evening before, a young fourteen-year-old boy and a friend had experimented with 251-NBOMe drug. The boy ended up jumping off a sixteen-floor balcony thinking he could fly. His friend took all his clothes off and ran down the street screaming all the way. He was hit by a car and was in critical condition in the hospital.'

'Will he survive?' Becky asked.

'I'm not sure, and we don't know what will be left of his brain cells after his episode. His parents are in shock. He's their only child. It's all so tragic – two young lives ruined by drugs. When will the kids listen to us?' he lamented as he pounded his fist on the soft sofa arm. 'I get so discouraged with what's happening in our society. I'm so glad that your children Ken and Sandy have their heads on straight and hopefully we can keep Mike from getting into trouble when he becomes older.' At this point he patted Becky's little baby mound, 'hopefully we will have these drugs under control by the time this little one gets old enough to be enticed by them.'

Becky was fully engrossed in editing a book, when Irma knocked on her office door. 'There's a phone call for you.'

'Who is it?' Becky asked.

'They didn't say,' she admitted shrugging her shoulders.

Becky took the phone and heard a man asking her to confirm that she was Rebecca Jeffries.

'Yes, I'm Rebecca Jeffries,' she admitted.

'I'm a representative of the Volunteer Edmonton Organization. We're having an awards day for volunteers who have excelled at what they do. You've been nominated for an award.'

'Does it say why I was nominated?' she asked.

'It says here that you're the project leader for the school talks about drugs that's sponsored by Crime Stoppers. I understand that they've been highly effective with the students,' he replied.

'Well, it's nice that I'm recognized, but it's the whole team that should be recognized.' Becky said.

'They can come along to the awards presentation – in uniform if possible, to show support for your cause,' he suggested.

'I'm sure that can be arranged. When will the ceremony be?'

'It's in two weeks' time,' and he gave Becky the address where it would be held. 'We'll be sending a letter to you that will confirm all the details. Congratulations on being nominated,' he concluded.

Becky phoned Mark with the news and he agreed to send out an e-mail to his volunteers to see how many could come to support Becky when she received the award.

That day arrived, and Becky was pleased that Dan was able to pop in to see and photograph her receiving the medal and award certificate. It was a lovely day, and Becky felt proud of her group as they rallied around her after the ceremony was over. One man came over to the group and asked how he could become a volunteer with them, and Mark took him aside to explain how he could apply.

Becky's medal and certificate were proudly placed by Irma on top of her china cabinet in their dining room. Irma gave her a big hug and beamed as she felt pride in her employer's volunteer award.

Chapter 7

When Becky went for her next check-up with her gynaecologist, he said, 'It's time for us to check your baby to see that everything's normal.'

Becky looked at him. She knew this time was coming and was scared that it might show she was carrying a defective child. The odds were higher for her because she was now close to forty. 'I've been dreading this,' Becky admitted.

'We now have two choices for checking your baby. The first is the well-known amniocentesis. Amniocentesis is performed to look for certain types of birth defects, such as Down syndrome, a chromosomal abnormality.'

'Because amniocentesis presents a small risk for both the mother and her baby, the prenatal test is generally offered to women who have a significant risk for genetic diseases, including those who have an abnormal ultrasound; have a family history of certain birth defects; have previously had a child or pregnancy with a birth defect; or will be thirty-five or older at the time of delivery. The latter reason is where you fit in.'

'You said there are two choices? What's the second one?' she queried.

Her doctor explained that during pregnancy, a mother's blood contains fragments of her baby's DNA.

He added that, 'The second test is a relatively new procedure. The test is called NIPT or non-invasive pre-natal testing which analyses the DNA in a sample of the mother's blood and poses no threat to the baby. It's used for women who are at least nine weeks pregnant and would like reassurance about the health of their unborn child. It's a non-invasive blood test that's safe for you and your baby. The test provides information about whether there's a high chance that your baby has a chromosome condition, such as Down syndrome. This tests ninety-nine percent of the chromosome conditions such as Trisomy 13 (Patau Syndrome), 18 (Edwards Syndrome) and 21 (Down syndrome), making it the most accurate test available. This NIPT test also screens for Monosomy X (Turner Syndrome) and Triploidy and will report those if they're detected. However, NIPT does not screen for all chromosomal abnormalities, nor does it screen for familial or inherited disorders (such as cystic fibrosis) or birth defects.

The First Trimester Screening (FTS) and NIPT are very different types of tests, both in how they test and the accuracy of their results. However, together they offer you very important information about the developing baby. FTS combines the results of blood tests with the ultrasound findings to predict the risk that the baby has a chromosomal or structural abnormality.

Here's a brochure that explains how it works. I'll leave you here and give you a chance to read it before you make a decision about which tests you would like to have.'

Becky read the brochure. It stated:

The NIPT test can provide an indication as to whether there is a high chance your baby has a chromosomal condition and can therefore help you decide whether further testing on the pregnancy itself, such as a chorionic villus sampling (CVS) or amniocentesis are tests that you want to pursue.

CVS is a pregnancy test that checks the baby for some genetic abnormalities such as Down syndrome and cystic fibrosis. A small sample of the placenta is taken via a needle and examined in a laboratory. The placenta is made of the same cells as the baby, so the baby can be tested by taking a small sample of the placenta. The sample is removed using a slender needle inserted through the abdomen. The tissue (chorionic villi) is then examined in a laboratory.

Unlike other pregnancy tests such as ultrasound, CVS isn't a general check of the baby's health but a specific test for particular abnormalities, such as Down syndrome or cystic fibrosis. The risk of miscarriage following CVS is one in a hundred, so it's important to thoroughly understand the benefits, risks and complications before agreeing to take the test. Generally, CVS is offered between ten- and nineteen-weeks' gestation.

Both CVS and amniocentesis are more invasive tests, and have associated risks, including the small chance of miscarriage.

The NIPT blood test is suitable for women who are at least nine weeks pregnant.

Becky was now in her tenth week of pregnancy, so she fit the requirements. When the doctor returned to her, she'd made her decision. 'I want the least invasive test possible. If the non-invasive test shows there's a problem, then I can have the amniocentesis and/or other tests.'

'Shall I set up a time for you to have it?' he asked.

She gulped and replied, 'I guess you'd better set it up.'

'I'll have our nurse set up an appointment for you to have the blood test. I'd like to see you early next week to discuss the results,' he added.

As Becky left the doctor's office, the nurse said, 'You're all set up at the pathology lab for next Friday morning at ten. Here's where you go for the blood test.'

That evening as they were getting ready for bed, Becky told Dan about the upcoming test. 'I'm really scared,' she admitted.

'I know you are. Do you want me to go with you when you have the test?' he said supportively.

'No, that's not necessary. It's only a blood test and I won't have the results until the next Tuesday. The doctor has made an appointment for me that day at eleven. That's when I'll likely need your support.'

'I'll ask for that time off. I don't want you to go through this alone. I'm pleased that we can start with a less invasive test. I've been a bit apprehensive about you having an amniocentesis test.

Becky had the blood test that Friday and then both she and Dan attended the doctor's appointment the next Tuesday. They both sat down apprehensively when it was time for them to speak with the doctor.

'I have good news,' he announced, knowing how concerned the couple must be. 'All the tests came back negative, so as far as we can see you have a healthy baby.'

Becky and Dan hugged each other. 'We're so relieved!' Becky admitted.

'I'd like to do an ultrasound to see how things are progressing. Do you want to know the sex of your baby?' he asked looking from one to the other.

'I'd rather not,' replied Becky and Dan agreed.

After her ultrasound showed that things were progressing nicely, the doctor said, 'Because of your earlier problems during your pregnancy, I'll want to see you every two weeks and later once every week until you deliver. How are you feeling generally?' he asked.

'I'm amazed at how much energy I have now that I'm over the morning sickness.' Becky admitted.

'Well, you must always caution yourself about overdoing it. You did hire someone to do the heavy work didn't you?' he asked with raised eyebrows.

'Yes. And she's a character, so helpful and fits in well with our family. I have her come three days a week right now and as I progress through the pregnancy, she'll come in five days a week.'

'Good. I'm counting on you to see that she does this,' he added as he looked at Dan.

'You bet. I'll be on her like a hound dog if I think she's overdoing it,' he promised.

Chapter 8

Becky was glad to have Irma's help, because she was so engrossed in editing a new book entitled 'Broken Dreams' written by a new author, Shirley Roberts. Shirley had been a battered wife, who after thirteen horrible years, had finally left her husband when he started to batter their children. Becky became engrossed in the story and couldn't put the manuscript down. It was well written - in the first person, so she felt as if she was there in person watching the events unfold. She took a break from reading the book to phone Jim, her boss at the publishing company.

'Hi Jim; it's Becky.'

'Well, hello little mother! How are you doing? We've missed you here in the office,' he expounded.

'Little mother isn't so little any more. I'm in my sixth month of pregnancy so am getting more and more awkward by the week. However, I feel fine and life is good,' she ended.

'Glad to hear that. How are things going with editing the new book I gave you?' he asked.

'That's what I wanted to talk to you about. Have you signed a publishing contract with Shirley?' she asked.

'We haven't finalized everything yet. We thought we'd wait till you had a chance to evaluate the book. Why do you ask?' he queried.

'Well, this is one of those books where we need to have the movie rights to it and every other right we can obtain to get it out there. It's bound to be a best-seller and has what it takes to make a block-buster movie as well,' she said excitedly.

'Have you spoken to Shirley about this?' he asked.

'No. I thought that was your department, but we need to move on this one. From what I've been able to establish, this is just part one of an even larger story and am wondering if she will be writing more about her life. If so, we should try to get the publishing rights for Shirley's next three or four books if possible.'

'Wow. You're really keen on this writer, aren't you?' he added.

'It's one of the best manuscripts I've read since starting with your company ten years ago,' she announced with a flourish.

'Well, I'll look into it today and will get back to you with what she says. I think my best approach is to prepare a publishing contract that includes all the areas we might need. When I talk to her about setting up an appointment, I'll ask her if she's writing anything more as a sequel to the first one. Then I'll get back to you,' he promised.

Becky was pleased when he phoned back a few hours later to confirm that Shirley was coming in to sign the contract. 'She was very surprised that we liked her book and kept saying that she'd never written a thing in her life before. I kept explaining that some people are natural writers who just need a good story to write about. She had not thought about writing more as a sequel to her first book but admitted that the book was only about her life with an abusive husband, but her life had turned around after she left him and from what she's told me – it's been a very unusual and interesting life,' he said excitedly.

'Everything in the book you're editing happened thirty years ago. I think I've encouraged her enough that she'll write more, and I hope she does. Well done, to have picked up on what a good writer she is. I had no idea how good she might be because she's a friend of one of our cover designers, and as a favour to her said we would look at the manuscript. I had no idea whether it would be good or not, so your endorsement of it is good enough for me to pull out all the stops.'

'Glad to hear that,' Becky replied. 'Has she designed a cover for the book?'

'I don't know whether she has or not. If she signs the publishing contracts, we might ask her friend, the cover designer, to come up with an appropriate cover, spine and possibly do the write-up for the back cover.'

Becky returned to the manuscript, making notations along the way to improve the context of the book. When she was finished editing it, she made a hard copy of the edited manuscript and prepared it to be couriered to Shirley. By this time Shirley had signed the publishing contract and the wheels were beginning to turn to get her book out there.

Once Shirley approved the changes, the book would be formatted for the size of book they wished to produce. Jim decided that because this would likely be a best-seller that they would start with a hard-cover edition, then a few months later would release the book in paperback format. He'd decided to make the paperback version larger than the average paperback book. Shirley's would be six inches by nine inches to make it stand out from other paperback books.

Jim phoned Becky when the hard-cover version was ready to be released. 'I know you can't do the book tour for the release of Shirley's book, so I've given that task to another of our editors. I hope you don't mind,' he said.

'I'm in no shape to even arrange a book tour let alone do one, and I'll be out of commission for at least six months after my little one is born. So, no, you're doing the right thing. However, I would like to keep in touch with Shirley to see how things are going for her, and of course want to be informed about book sales. Possibly when the paperback version comes out, I might be able to do another book tour with her and arrange for the television, radio and newspaper interviews.'

'I'll keep that in mind when we're ready to release the paperback. If the hard-cover book goes well enough, we may hold off doing the paperback and eBook editions for longer than usual. By then you should be ready to take it on.'

'Do you think we could get someone interested in doing a movie about the book?' she asked.

'I think we'll wait till the hard-cover is well launched before I do that. I think we'll then have several movie groups vying for it,' he surmised.

'That sounds like a good plan. I have a really good feeling about this book – I think it will go far,' she ended.

Chapter 9

Before Dan and Becky were married, his ex-wife Emily had been in a serious car accident and was left paralysed from the waist down. At that time, she had custody of their two-year-old son Mike, with weekend visits to Dan. All that changed after her accident. She was in the hospital for a month, then in rehabilitation for another month. When she was released from the rehabilitation centre, she went to live with her parents. In the meantime, she made the decision that Dan would have the major custody of their son Mike. It was a mutual agreement and Dan went out of his way to ensure that Emily would have regular visits with their son.

Because of his erratic hours working with the police, and the growing affection between the Becky and Dan, they decided to move in together, but soon realized that their existing homes were too small for their extended family. They couldn't believe their luck when they found a lovely older home in the same neighbourhood where Becky lived. They'd fixed it up and settled into the four-bedroom home. The children had their own bedrooms, and they were able to use the fourth bedroom as an office. This is where Becky spent much of her time editing her books now that she was working out of their home.

While Emily was recuperating from her accident, she decided to take art classes and began dabbling at painting and sketching. She was very surprised to find that she was good at it, so continued taking classes to improve her ability. As she became more accomplished, she was pleased that she was able to sell a few of her paintings. In only a year, she seemed to have an innate ability to take what she saw and put it down on paper. She was especially good at charcoal drawings. One weekend when Mike stayed with her and her parents, she made several sketches of him. When Dan came to pick him up on Sunday evening, she showed them to him.

'These are terrific!' he exclaimed. 'Would you give one or two of them to me? I'd love to have them and can get them framed.'

'Sure. You can have them all. I'll do more the next time he's here for the weekend,' she promised.

'Do you have any more things you've done?' he asked. He'd had no idea she was this good.

She showed him a few watercolours and a tiny one that was her first oil attempt. 'It's harder painting with oils – if you make a mistake, it's harder to correct,' she admitted.

'These are really good. You have a rare talent,' he said as he congratulated her.

When he brought the three sketches of Mike home and showed them to Becky, she looked in wonder at them then stated, 'We've got to frame these. I'll take them to a framing place and see what kind of frame they would recommend for a charcoal sketch.'

By the end of the week, the three sketches were proudly displayed on their living room wall.

Several weeks later, Dan delivered Mike to Emily's parents' home as usual, and was surprised when Emily asked if he could stay for a little while. Her mother had made some cinnamon buns and offered him a cup of coffee, then left the room. Dan knew that there was something new in the wind and wondered what was up.

'As you know, I've been taking physio to keep my legs as supple as possible, but lately my doctors have had me trying a new treatment called biofeedback. This is where you use your mind to control your body in new ways. It's often used for migraine headaches, chronic pain and for people recovering from strokes. My doctor thought I had nothing to lose by trying it. Here's an article that explains how it works,' she concluded as she handed him an information sheet about bio-feedback.

Biofeedback operates on the notion that we have the innate ability and potential to influence the automatic functions of our bodies through the exertion of will and mind. Biofeedback has recently been shown to give us what had previously seemed an impossible degree of control over a variety of physiologic events.

Biofeedback is based on the idea, confirmed by scientific studies, that people have the innate potential to influence with their minds many of the automatic, involuntary functions of their bodies. To help patients develop this ability, a biofeedback specialist uses signals from special monitoring equipment to teach patients how to control certain body functions and their responses, such as: brain activity, blood pressure, muscle tension, heart rate, skin temperature, and sweat gland activity.

You can receive biofeedback training in physical therapy clinics, medical centres and hospitals. A growing number of feedback devices and programs are being marketed for home use as well, but working with a therapist, initially, may provide the best long-term results.

Preparation depends on the type of biofeedback therapy used. A typical biofeedback session lasts thirty to sixty minutes. The length and number of sessions will be determined by your condition and how quickly you learn to control your physical responses.

During a biofeedback session, a therapist will apply electrical sensors to different parts of your body. These sensors will monitor your body's physiological response to stress - for instance, your muscle contraction during a tension headache - then feed the information back to you via cues such as a beeping sound or a flashing light. The feedback will allow you to begin to associate your body's response - in this case, headache pain - with certain physical functions, such as your muscles tensing.

Once you begin to recognise that your headache is a result of tense muscles, the next step is to learn how to invoke positive physical changes in your body, such as relaxing those specific muscles when your body is physically or mentally stressed. Your eventual goal will be to produce these responses on your own, outside the therapist's office and without the help of technology.

Experts aren't entirely sure how the biofeedback therapy works. Many people who've tried it can't explain how they're able to control their bodies, yet experience improvement in their symptoms.

When Dan finished reading the information, he looked at Emily with a questioning look.

'Dan, it's working a bit with me and I'm getting some sensation back in my feet. It's not much, but the doctors are very happy that even that much progress has been made. I wanted you to know about this, because if I can again become independent, you know I'll want to have Mike back on a permanent basis,' she announced watching Dan's reaction.

Dan shifted in his chair. This was a new development. His son Mike had moved in with his new family a year ago after Emily's accident, and he would not want Mike to go back to living full-time with Emily. He decided to touch on the subject.

'We've all become adjusted to having Mike with us and know it would be hard for us to let him go. Possibly when the time comes and you're able to look after him again, we might have split custody with both of us having the same access to Mike.'

'I'll have to think about that,' Emily replied. She knew that she might not be able to be fully independent, but knew she wanted her son to be back with her as soon as possible. 'Let's see how my treatments go and how far I progress. I think that's the most important thing for me to concentrate on right now,' she concluded.

Dan nodded his head. He certainly hoped that she would regain full function of her legs, but as he looked down at them, he could see that they had withered away considerably in the past year and wondered whether in fact she could regain the use of them. 'I guess it's a matter of us seeing what progress you make.'

As he left their home, he nodded to Emily's mother who patted his arm and said, 'Isn't it wonderful that she might walk again?'

'Yes, that would certainly be wonderful, but you must keep her grounded. This improvement might only go so far, then stop progressing. Her injury was so serious that she may only be able to go so far in renewing the neurons in her body.'

He waved as he left the home. 'I'll be back on Sunday night to collect Mike as usual.'

When he got home, Becky could see that he was troubled. 'Is everything all right?' she asked as she kissed his cheek. 'You look upset.'

'I guess I am. I've learned about something that could again change our lifestyle.' Then he explained about his talk with Emily.

Becky was taken aback. She had never heard about bio-feedback and was apprehensive that it could be so powerful a treatment that Emily would walk again. 'Why don't we look this up on the web and see what it says about biofeedback?' she suggested.

Dan nodded, then both went to their computers and did a web search to see what they could find. Here's what Becky found in an article explaining what biofeedback can be used for:

There is a whole range of health conditions that experts believe can be treated with biofeedback therapy. In fact, it is a very popular choice over drugs, because it does not have any significant risks or cause undesirable side effects.

Other benefits of biofeedback therapy are that it is noninvasive and can be an alternative to medications, which is particularly useful for pregnant women.

During a biofeedback session, electrodes are attached to your skin. Finger sensors can also be used. These electrodes/sensors send signals to a monitor, which displays a sound, flash of light, or image that represents your heart and breathing rate, blood pressure, skin temperature, sweating, or muscle activity.'

Dan looked up from his computer and read from another article he'd found:

Impairment from strokes involve both the decreased force of muscle contraction and dysfunctional contractions known as spaciticy. The contraction of several closely grouped muscles, instead of controlling the contraction and relaxation of individual muscles, cause spaciticy.

Strokes can affect the functions of the shoulder, wrist-hand and ankle joints resulting in weakness of the rotator cuff in the shoulder joint that are dependent on the muscles for normal movement. The stroke patient, through the readings provided by the biofeedback apparatus can gain conscious control over subliminal yet undamaged upper neuron pathways which are in turn able to replace the missing functions responsible for the altered physical ability. This does not replace physiotherapy but enhances the results. Some patients cite rather dramatic and remarkable recoveries from what were thought to be permanent disabilities. Case studies described instances where patients, thought to have long since plateaued in their rehabilitation course, discarded their braces and walked away almost unaided.'

'It sounds as if Emily is one of those people who are being helped by biofeedback. This explains her remarkable progress. I must show this to her and encourage her to keep up her physiotherapy,' Dan said emphatically.

He telephoned Emily and told her the web pages to go to for the information they'd found, especially the information they found about stroke victims.

'Thanks Dan. I found something similar myself a few days ago. I think I'm one of the lucky ones who might recover full function. However, my doctor says that I can have set-backs later during my life when the new neuron pathways become fatigued, so he's advised me not to overdo things from now on and to listen to my body when it tells me I've done enough. That will be hard to do because I'm so stoked about the progress I've made.'

Then she added, 'Thanks for your support Dan. You don't know how important that will be as I keep working to regain full mobility.'

They hung up, both with smiles on their faces knowing she had a good chance to recover at least some of her movements. Dan and Becky shut down their computers feeling good that they had helped her at least a bit.

Emily continued practising her biofeedback and went full-on with her physiotherapy. Week by week, she improved and was able to do more things for herself around the home. She could pull herself out of her wheelchair, and hanging onto a counter or piece of furniture, manipulate herself around a room without help. She still did not have the balance to hold Mike except when she was sitting but hoped that if she kept up her treatment that she would be able to do that as well. She was very anxious for that to happen because she wanted her son back with her.

Chapter 10

Becky was editing a book in early November when her phone rang. It was her friend Brenda Walker. She'd met Brenda when they'd both taken self-defence courses and had become good friends. Brenda had been her maid of honour last June when she and Dan were married.

'Hi Becky. How are things?' Brenda asked.

'Doing well. I'm getting bigger and bigger, but I feel healthy. How are you?' she queried.

'Well... I have some news!' she tempted.

'Oh, and what would that be?' Becky knew that Brenda and her boyfriend Fred Connolly were close, so wasn't surprised when Brenda gushed, 'I'm getting married!'

'I'm not surprised,' replied Becky. 'When do you think you'll get married?'

'We're romantics and have chosen to get married on Valentine's day.'

'Sounds good. Will your wedding be here in Edmonton?' Becky asked.

'Yes. We want a quiet wedding with only a few friends there to celebrate with us,' she explained, and then added, 'I'd like you to be my matron of honour.'

'Oh, I don't know about that. I'll be as big as a whale by then. Over six months pregnant in fact,' Becky said with emphasis.

'That won't matter. We can choose a dress that's flattering and who cares whether you're pregnant or not – you're my best friend,' she confirmed.

'Well, as long as you don't care how big I am – you're on. I'll be your matron of honour,' she agreed.

'Great. We'll wait until after Christmas to pick out your outfit. You can choose what colour and style you want, because I won't have any other bridesmaids or a flower girl. We do want to keep it simple.'

'Will your Dad be able to give you away?' Becky asked. She knew that Brenda's parents were divorced and hated each other.

'Yes. I'll be asking him a bit later and of course will invite his new wife to come with him. My Mom has been such a bitch during the separation and divorce that I doubt if she will come to the wedding if my Dad's there - especially if his wife comes with him. I don't really care. Mom and I have never been close – always on a different page in life. It will be a shame if she doesn't come, but it will be her choice. I'll have to phone her soon to tell her about the wedding and give her time to decide whether she'll come or not.'

'I'm sorry you have to face all that turmoil. Weddings are supposed to be happy affairs, and it's often family members who can make things difficult for everyone. I hope she's adult enough to come to the wedding,' she concluded.

'I do too. How about we get together next week, and you can help me pick out a wedding dress?' said Brenda, welcoming the chance to change the subject.

'That will be fine with me. I'll see if Emily will look after Mike that day, or possibly get my neighbour Mary to so.' They made a time to get together and discussed all the stores they would go to that sold wedding dresses.

Brenda had a lovely, sculptured body and was in wonderful physical shape, so she chose a slim-line tulle mid-calf length dress with a sweetheart neckline. It was a very sexy dress, but suited Brenda to a tee.

In the coming weeks, Brenda often consulted Becky about wedding procedure, and since it had only been a few months since her wedding, she was able to keep Brenda on track to ensure that everything would be ready for her special day.

Chapter 11

Becky and Dan invited Brenda and Fred to their home for Christmas dinner. On Christmas Eve day, Irma had followed the list Becky had made and purchased all the items required for the feast. Just before she left on Christmas Eve, she prepared the turkey, so it would be ready for Dan to put into the oven for Becky on Christmas morning. She knew that this was something that Becky should not do because it was a big turkey and was heavy.

That evening the family sat around the Christmas tree singing carols. Mike added his little voice and had them in stitches because he ad-libbed most of the words. Some of them were highly inappropriate for a Christmas carol. He thought this was great fun and joined in even more.

Dan's cell phone rang, and Becky watched as his face blanched of colour and knew from the intense look on his face that something was going down with the police.

'I'll be right there,' he said as he closed his phone. He turned to Becky and asked if she could join him in their bedroom. He didn't want his children to hear what he had to say.

'An Islamic terrorist group has just made a bomb threat. They say they've placed several bombs in West Edmonton Mall that are set to be detonated just after midnight, so they can celebrate Christmas in their own way. I've got to go right away,' he said as he unlocked his gun safe, retrieved his gun, put it into his holster and struggled into his bullet-proof vest. Then he put on his suit jacket and warm winter coat.

Becky gave him a worried look, but knew he had to go. She reached up and gave him a big hug and kiss, hoping that he would not be injured if the bombs did indeed go off. She leaned heavily against the door after Dan left their home, took a big breath before joining her children.

Sandy knew something was wrong, but said instead, 'Why don't I get Mike ready for bed and read him a story, then we can talk.'

Becky nodded her head and sat down on the sofa. It had been such a lovely night. Why did those terrible people have to spoil special events such as these? How could they have no compassion for others, and instead take pleasure on torturing others and making their lives as miserable as possible? 'What did we ever do to them to make them this volatile that they lash out at anyone who is not of their religion? How dare they!'

She then thought. 'Enough is enough – leave us alone and go back to your own country if you want to shed blood. Shed your own blood – not ours!'

She was crying by this time. 'What a terrible world it's turned out to be with such radical people in our midst. Why does our government not turf them all out – they cause only problems for others. They left their own countries because of the conflict and instead of being peaceful people, they start their own wars here. Go, please go!'

Sandy finished tucking Mike into bed and read him a short story. He knew that tomorrow Santa would come and kept asking her what he was going to bring him.

'You'll have to go to sleep – because Santa won't come if you're awake. So, settle down and go to sleep,' she said as she left the door a bit ajar.

She joined her mother in the living room. The Christmas tree lights gave the room a warm glow, but all she could see on Becky's face was anguish. 'What's happening,' she asked her mom as she put her arm around her shoulders.

'It's as serious as it gets. The police have received a bomb threat from an Islamic group, saying that the West Edmonton

Mall has several bombs that will be detonated at midnight, so it will spoil everyone's Christmas celebrations,' she explained sadly.

'The idiots. Why don't they go home and cause problems there? We don't want you!' she almost shouted as she looked at the door pointing with her finger that they should leave.

'Yes, it's a sad world we live in when these kinds of people are out there. They have been warring with each other for over two thousand years, and now they're doing it here. It makes me so sad, and more so because it's putting your Dad in danger. That's where he's gone, and I just hope he'll be all right,' she added sadly.

'I feel the same Mom. I hope Dad can keep in touch with us, but guess he'll be very busy with the other policemen trying to find the bombs.'

Dan arrived at the staging point near the mall and learned that Marshall law had been implemented. Army personnel were swarming the mall with bomb detectors and twenty sniffer dogs were searching the complex, but it was so huge that it was a monumental task. The Fantasyland Hotel had been evacuated and people were being transported by bus to other hotel accommodations. The management of the shopping complex were kept busy finding keys, so they could check all the stores and restaurants in the complex. They knew they would not have time to check everything in the three hours they had until the midnight deadline.

Edmonton Police Service personnel were given the task of containing the perimeter of the complex with two police officers at every entrance to the complex including the staff entrances. Dan was situated near the Fantasyland Hotel and kept a watchful eye on anything that moved near the hotel. The hours went by and Dan was very cold. He and his partner John Knight took turns going inside the entrance of the hotel to warm up. Dan had just returned to his post when he saw some movement near an enclosed taxi stand about ten metres away from the entrance. He quietly let John know that he'd seen some movement, and they both used their peripheral vision to see if they could see any more movement.

'You're right – there's someone there, John whispered. 'I'll walk out into the parking lot using my flashlight and shine it near the taxi stand which should divert the person enough that you can move closer to him.'

Dan moved until he was on the other side of the taxi stand and saw his partner swinging his flashlight in a sweeping motion getting closer and closer to the taxi stand, but not close enough to make the man feel he was on to him. There was just enough room behind the taxi stand for Dan to slowly move sideways behind it until he was able to see the man crouched down to the right of him. Dan stepped out from behind the bin, took the stance, holding his gun in two hands and shouted for the man to get on the ground.

The man immediately spun around, still crouching and Dan saw he had a gun in his hand. They both shot at the same time.

The man was flung onto his back and was busy trying with his left hand to get something out of the right pocket of his jacket. John was there in a few seconds and grabbed his left hand, handcuffed it to a railing around the taxi stand and carefully withdrew the item from his pocket. It was a cell phone.

John quickly examined Dan and saw two wounds on his head that were bleeding heavily. His immediate thought was, 'Oh God, Dan's had a head shot. He's finished.'

Chapter 12

Becky hadn't been able to settle down knowing Dan could be hurt during this terrible event. She made herself a cup of tea and picked up a novel to try to keep herself diverted. From time to time, she watched the news bulletins as they interrupted the regular viewing. Then they announced that there was an officer down, and somehow Becky knew it was Dan. But what could she do? She knew she had to wait until someone identified the officer, or someone phoned her with the news, so she wasn't surprised when the phone call came.

Back at West Edmonton Mall, John called into the command post that there was an officer down. He added that a man had been apprehended and was also shot, so they needed two ambulances as soon as possible. Within minutes the police officer in charge of the event arrived and two ambulances. The ambulances had been on stand-by a few blocks away because of the bomb situation, so John was glad they were able to attend to Dan right away.

The second ambulance personnel examined the prisoner and determined that he'd just had a shoulder injury on his gun hand. They found the man's gun and the police chief was given the mobile phone.

The chief asked the paramedics where they would take the injured men, then barked out, 'John, I want you to go in the ambulance with the man you apprehended,' then turning to another man, he said, 'Officer Miller, I want you to very carefully take this mobile phone to the bomb experts to see if they can disarm it if it's programmed to set off a bomb.' Then he snapped to another two officers, 'I want you two to take over this post at the front of the Fantasyland Hotel. Officer Jacobs, I want you to phone Dan's wife and let her know that her husband has been shot,' he concluded.

So, it was Officer Jacobs who had the terrible task of informing Becky that Dan had been shot.

It was shortly after eleven, when the phone rang, Becky steeled herself knowing that this might be the call that all police officer's families did not want to hear. 'Hello, this is Officer Jacobs of the Edmonton Police Service. May I please speak with Rebecca Jeffries?'

'I'm Becky Jeffries,' she confirmed.

'I'm sorry to tell you that your husband Dan has been shot and is on his way to the Royal Alexandra Hospital. Do you wish to have me pick you up or can you make it to the hospital yourself?'

'We live not far from the hospital, so I can drive there,' she said in a quiet voice.

'Will you be okay to drive?' he asked, rather worried about her because he knew she was pregnant.

'Yes,' she agreed taking a big breath. 'I'll be fine.'

Sandy had just gone to bed, so Becky told her what had happened. Becky knew she was lying when she assured her that Dan would be all right. As Becky was driving to the hospital, she couldn't help but wonder what she would do if Dan died. How would she be able to support her family? What would the children do without a father? Would Mike move back permanently with Emily?' Then, she realized that because Dan had been shot while on duty, he would have death benefit for the family.

'What am I thinking these thoughts for,' she said as she shook her head at the thought of losing Dan. 'I have got to remain positive!'

They'd told her he'd been shot but didn't tell her that it looked like a head wound that could be fatal. All she knew was that he'd been shot.

In the meantime, two other suspects had been apprehended. Two plain clothed policemen had been given the task of evacuating a nearby restaurant in case a bomb did go off. As they walked towards the restaurant, they noticed two men who never took their eyes of the mall. Everyone else in the restaurant seemed to be having conversations, but they were rigidly focused on what was transpiring at the mall. One of the officers quietly asked to speak with the manager. He showed him his badge and quietly warned him that his restaurant had to be evacuated immediately.

His partner had been looking around the restaurant and was glad that there were only a few people enjoying a meal. Then his gaze went to the two men who were still focused on the mall. In each of their hands was a mobile phone. He nodded to his partner and they each rushed over to the men and snatched the mobile phones out of their hands and handed them to the manager. 'Be careful with these,' one said. Then the two of them hauled the two men out of the booth and cuffed them. As they patted them down, they found that one had an ankle holster for his gun and the other had a switch-blade knife in his pocket.

The bomb squad now had three mobile phones to examine and disable.

The army personnel were busy sweeping the building and had been successful in finding three bombs but had no idea how many there might be in total, so hoped that the mobile phones might be for some that were still hidden. As it got closer and closer to midnight, the search intensified, and a fourth bomb was discovered and disarmed.

In the ambulance, Dan was examined by the paramedics. He was bleeding in two areas of his head. One was from a wound and huge bump on the back of his head and another was from a bleeding gash on his forehead. Like most head wounds, there was a considerable amount of blood. Initially the paramedics thought he had been struck by a bullet that had gone through his brain but were very relieved to determine that the force of being hit by the bullet had smashed him back against the brick wall of the building with tremendous force knocking him unconscious. Then he hit his head again when he fell lifelessly to the pavement. They searched for a gunshot wound but couldn't find one. They then rushed him to the hospital to deal with his head wounds.

When Becky arrived at the hospital she paced back and forth in the admitting room until she was able to speak with the young doctor who'd examined Dan.

'He has a concussion from two bashes on his head. We thought for a while that the wounds were entrance and exit wounds from a gunshot, but they were from his head impacting on the building wall and on the concrete – so he has two nasty bumps.'

He sat down next to Becky noting that she was pregnant and wanted to assure her that her husband did not have life-threatening injuries. 'We've had a chance to undress him and remove the bullet-proof vest he was wearing. We discovered that there is a dint in the vest where he must have been hit almost point blank by the bullet fired at him. Under the vest is a huge bruise on his chest, but none of the bones have been broken. He'll have a sore chest for a week or two before that heals. What we need to concentrate on now is the concussion. We'll be monitoring him closely for that. I'll keep you informed. Do you have any questions?'

Becky thanked the doctor and asked whether she could sit with Dan.

'Yes, you can. In fact, if you see him waking up or moving around at all, please let us know. In the meantime, can the nurses get you a cup of tea or coffee?' he asked kindly.

'I would love a cup of tea – I'm rather stressed out over this and wonder what's happening at the West Edmonton Mall,' she added.

'I've been informed that there've been several bombs removed from the premises,' he said as he looked up at the clock. 'The bombs were set to go off at midnight and I see that it's now past that. I wonder how things have transpired? I hope they got them all and that the terrorists have all been caught.'

'So do I,' agreed Becky.

Becky was sipping her cup of tea when John arrived. He had been relieved of his duty of watching the criminal Dan had shot. As he approached Becky, he said, 'I was Dan's partner tonight,' he explained. 'Everyone is worried about him. How is he?'

'Thankfully, the bullet hit his vest and has caused a huge bruise on his sternum, but it's the concussion from him being flung back into the wall of the building plus hitting the pavement with his head that are the problems. The doctor says all they can do right now is keep checking his vitals and watching for him to become conscious again,' she added.

'I can't tell you how relieved I am. I thought the injuries on his head were from a head shot – an entrance and exit wound. I have to be honest, I thought he was a goner or would end up brain damaged.' Then he added, 'This must be a trying time for you especially since this is now officially Christmas day. You'll always remember this Christmas I imagine.' he said sadly.

'Speaking about it being Christmas – do you have a family you should be with right now?' she asked him.

'Yes, my wife and possibly my daughter might still be awake wondering if I've been hurt at the site. I must give them a call and tell them I'm okay, but I wanted to see how Dan was before I contacted them.'

'Do call them, but also - if you're off duty - please go home. If Dan gets worse, I promise I'll phone you. Please give me your home number and in any case, I'll call you in the morning about his condition.'

'Okay, thanks,' he said, glad that he would be able to go home to his family.

Earlier, Becky had phoned Sandy who answered the phone right away, so Becky knew she'd not been sleeping. 'Your Dad is better than we thought,' she said then described how the vest had saved his life and that they just had to wait for him to wake up. She encouraged Sandy to go to sleep, so she would be wide awake enough to care for Mike if she had to stay at the hospital with Dan.

It was shortly after two when Becky saw some movement from Dan. He put his hand on his chest and grimaced with his face. He was probably remembering being hit in the chest and felt the impact.

Then he suddenly opened his eyes and sat up in bed, ready to defend himself.

'Dan, Dan,' she said as she restrained him. 'You're okay. It's all over. You're okay.'

She peered into his eyes and saw the terror in them. 'Was I shot?' he asked, looking wide-eyed around the room.

'Yes, you were, but your vest saved you. You'll just have a huge bruise from that, but no broken bones.'

He rubbed his head, 'Then why do I feel so awful? I feel like I might throw up,' he said as his face took on a greenish tinge.

Becky grabbed the kidney shaped dish and held it out to him and helped him get onto his side. At the same time, she pushed the call button for the nurse who took over and helped Dan as he vomited.

'This is quite usual with concussion,' the nurse explained. 'It's because concussion can cause a bit of vertigo that can upset a person's stomach. I'll get you something for the nausea,' she added as she added an extra pillow and raised his bed a little. She handed a clean kidney basin to Becky and left the room to get the anti-nausea medicine. She returned and put the medicine into the canula with the saline solution already dripping into Dan's body.

She waited a few minutes then asked Dan, 'Do you feel a little less nauseous now?'

He nodded his head, then winced as he put his hand to one of the big bandages on his head. He felt around his head a bit then said, 'I can feel two huge bumps. What did I do, hit myself with my own gun?'

'No, you were thrown back onto the building wall by the force of the shot. That knocked you unconscious, and then you fell to the hard, frozen pavement and hit your head again. So, you did a good job on your head.'

'How long will I have to be here?' he asked the nurse.

'Until we're sure you're okay, she replied. 'I would think that you'll be here for at least a day or two.'

'Oh no! How about Christmas?' he asked remembering what day it was.

'I'm afraid your family will have to come here to be with you. We don't want you to leave till we're sure you're okay,' the nurse confirmed.

Dan looked at Becky then glanced at the clock. His eyes widened as he asked, 'What's happened at the West Edmonton Mall? Did they get all the bombs?'

Becky shrugged her shoulders and said, 'I really don't know what's happened there. I've been with you with no access to television.'

That was the moment when Dan's police chief entered the room. He was glad to see that Dan was conscious and looking much better than he had at the site of the shooting. He also thought Dan was going to die.

'I can answer that question for you. We must have found them all - because none blew up. You were able to stop one of the men who had mobile phones. If your man had pushed a certain button, it would have blown up a bomb, so you and several other officers are heroes. There were two other men apprehended by our police and we disarmed their mobile phones. The bomb squad dogs were able to find several bombs and they were also dismantled. So, everyone did a good job, and the terrorists lost out on this one. We have three men in custody and we're checking the contents of their mobile phones for other contacts.'

'That's a relief. The last thing I remember was him turning around and pointing his gun at me. We were only about a metre away from each other, so I thought I was going to die when I heard his gun discharge.'

'Well, you shot him at the same time and John was able to get his mobile phone before he was able to detonate his bomb. Well done by the two of you,' he added as he shook Dan's hand.

Becky could see Dan flush. He wasn't a man who wanted glory; he just wanted the crooks caught. 'What will happen to the men you've apprehended?'

'First of all, they will be charged with terrorism, and the one who shot you will be charged with attempted murder. You will have to testify at his trial, but that won't be for quite some time while we look into seeing who else was involved.'

'Were they Canadians?' Dan asked.

'Yes, all three were Canadian citizens, but all three were born in the Middle East and were Muslim,' the police chief stated.

'Why, oh why, do we let them into our country?' asked Dan.

The police chief just shook his head and added, 'I must get back to the missus. She's probably sitting up waiting for me, but I had to check to see how you were doing first. You and the man you shot were the only serious injuries during this raid. I'm so glad about that especially at this time of the year. And by the way - Merry Christmas!'

He waved as he left the room. Dan looked at Becky, yawned, then said, 'I don't know about you, but I'm pooped. Why don't you go home? I'm going to be okay. Do you think you can bring the kids some time tomorrow morning?'

'Sure I will. I'll let them open their gifts, then we can bring yours up to the hospital for you to open – or should I say Mike will open them for you,' she laughed.

'Sounds like a good plan. I'd promised Emily that I would bring Mike over for Christmas dinner late in the afternoon, and he was going to spend the night there. Could you see that he gets there – possibly after you visit me with the kids?'

'I'll arrange that. I'll phone Emily in the morning and bring her up to date about your condition. In the meantime, you have as good a sleep as you can with your headache.' She leaned over and kissed him gently then added emotionally, 'I'm so glad you're safe – what would I do without you.'

He squeezed her hand and blinked away a tear of his own.

That morning Mike was his usual busy self and woke Sandy and Becky with the news that 'Santa's come! Santa's come! Let's open our presents!' as he dragged them both out of bed. Both were tired because they'd only had a few hours sleep but knew that Christmas was for kids and here was a very excited little one.

Mike asked why Dan wasn't home and they had to tell him that he had hit his head and was in the hospital. Mike put his hands on his hips and pouted, 'Then we should take all these things,' and his hand swept over all the gifts displayed under the tree, 'and take them up to the hospital.'

'Well, we'll be going to see your Dad, but he wants us to open our presents here first, then take his up to the hospital. Will that be all right with you?' Becky asked.

'I guess so,' he said with a pouty look, 'But Dad won't see us open them!'

'Well let's open our presents!' said Sandy as she raced Mike to the tree. They were kept busy opening gifts. Becky got a big box and they put Dan's presents into it as they came to them under the tree. Soon the living room was full of wrapping paper and gifts, and Becky called them into the kitchen to have their breakfast.

'Will we be going up to see Dad now?' asked Mike,

'Yes, sweetheart, we'll go as soon as I clean up from breakfast.'

Then she remembered that Brenda and Fred had been invited to share Christmas dinner with them. It was obvious that Brenda had been asleep but became instantly alert when Becky explained what had happened the night before.

'Don't worry about us coming to dinner. We can make other plans. Fred and I will be spending most of the day with his parents and they too had invited us for dinner, so we can go there instead.'

'I'm glad you can make other plans. I really don't know what will happen for dinner today. Which reminds me; my son Ken is coming too. I'd better phone him to let him know about his step-father.'

'Give Dan a kiss from me,' said Brenda as they said goodbye.

When Becky phoned Ken, he said he would be coming anyway. He had a key to the house, so would phone her when he arrived.

Dan's face lit up when his family came to his room, shortly after ten that morning. He had a beautiful shiner and bruise on his forehead from when he hit the pavement and the lump on the back of his head was giving him a terrible headache. Just before they arrived, the nurse had given him a shot to help him deal with the pain of it all.

He was out of the intensive care unit and in a room of his own by then and had phoned Becky to tell her about the room change. Sandy and Mike lugged the box of his gifts into the room and made a big thing out of giving Dan each gift. Mike took his shoes off and crawled into bed with his dad and 'helped' him open his gifts.

Several people went by in the hallway singing Christmas carols and it was a lovely time they spent together. Soon it was time to go and by this time Dan was sagging. They gathered up his gifts, except for a book that Dan wanted to keep so he had something to read. They all gave Dan a hug and off they went.

The hospital would not let people use mobile phones on their premises, and when Becky got to her car, she saw that there was a message waiting for her from Ken.

'Should I come up to the hospital?' he asked when she called him.

'Not now,' she said and explained that Dan was tired and planned to sleep a bit. 'We're on our way to deliver Mike to Emily's place and will be home after that. Maybe you could come up to see him tonight. I know I'll be too tired, because both Sandy and I were up most of the night.'

'Good idea. By the way, Irma's here. She must have arrived just after you left for the hospital and you'll have your turkey dinner as planned.'

'Please thank Irma for doing that for us. What a gem she is!'

'You've got that right' he agreed.

Becky delivered Mike to Emily's home and Sandy was surprised when Emily gave her a gift. She had not expected one and didn't have one for Emily, so she was a bit embarrassed.

'Thanks Emily. I didn't expect a gift. That was nice of you,' she said as she gave Emily a hug.

When they arrived home Becky said, 'Oh Irma, thanks so much for doing this for us. Please stay for dinner and keep us company.'

'I heard on the radio that Dan had been hurt and have kept in touch with the hospital. I'm glad he's better, but sorry he couldn't be home for Christmas dinner. Maybe you can take him some of this to him later,' she added.

'Will you stay and have dinner with us?' added Sandy. It was going to be a quiet Christmas dinner without Dan and Mike.

'I'd love to stay,' Irma replied. She was a widow and lived alone and was not looking forward to spending the evening alone. She was glad she had the opportunity of helping them by fixing the dinner she'd helped prepare. She was glad she had a key to their home, so she'd been able to enter the home and fix their dinner.

Becky was tempted to prepare a plate of dinner for Ken to take to the hospital but realized that Dan had likely already had his dinner. She decided that if he was still in the hospital the next day, she'd take him a plate of food for his meal.

Dan was sitting in a chair in his room and was glad to see Ken who explained that he'd come alone because Becky and Sandy had been up most of the night.

'I'm glad your mom didn't come. She needs to take it easy and the past twenty hours couldn't have been easy on her.

The next morning Dan's doctor released him from the hospital but insisted that he spend a week to ten days at home recuperating. When Dan got home, he took Becky aside and said, 'With me having to take these days off – what do you say we take Sandy to Hawaii until I have to go back to work? I'm sure Emily and her family would love to keep Mike if we were to go.'

'Will your doctor allow you to fly?' Becky asked, thinking of his health first. 'And I'd better check with mine to make sure it will be okay for me to fly now that I'm almost five months pregnant.'

Dan replied, 'I never thought to ask about my own condition, but I guess with a head injury it could have some impact if I was at a different altitude. I'll call him and see what he says, and hopefully your doctor will say it's okay for you to go as well.' Dan agreed.

They spoke with their respective doctors. Dan's doctor thought it would be fine for him to go to Hawaii; in fact, he thought it might be a good idea for him to have a fully relaxing time in the sun. Becky's doctor approved as well, as long as she took it easy and didn't do too much. Edmonton winter that year had been extremely cold and everyone who could do so, had headed towards warmer climates.

Dan then talked to Emily who agreed to keep Mike. When all that had been arranged, Becky went on the internet to see if there were any last-minute flights and hotel reservations they could make. They were in luck, but they could not sit together on the plane. Because they did not want Sandy to sit alone, she sat with Dan to keep an eye on him and Becky sat a few rows behind them.

They had a wonderful week at the beach in Kihei, but Dan was careful to wear a tee shirt when he went to the beach because of the horrible bruise he had all over his chest from the bullet hitting his vest. Slowly but surely the bruising on his forehead and the back of his head also subsided, but he found he had to take painkillers for several days because of the headaches he suffered. Before he left Edmonton, his doctor had e-mailed him a letter and given him the name of an excellent doctor on Maui in case he required medical help.

They were there over New Years and Dan took Becky to a lovely restaurant where they did several slow dances. When it was midnight, he kissed her softly and said, 'Happy New Year darling. It's going to be such a good year and I'm going to be a daddy soon!' he said as he quietly patted her growing tummy. They left shortly after everyone sang Old Lang Syne.

The three of them came back to Edmonton rested and refreshed after the quick holiday. Sandy loved it because it was her first trip to Hawaii.

Their first task when they got home was to pick Mike up at Emily's. Mike was a non-stop talker as they drove to their home, telling them all the things he'd done while they were away. He also told them that his Mommy was able to stand up a bit and everyone had been clapping and happy when that happened.

Soon it was time for them all to get back to their normal lives. Dan went back to work - Becky went back to editing her books and Sandy returned to school. Dan and Becky had decided that Irma should now come in five days a week so that Becky would not have to do any strenuous work at all. Irma doted on her, bringing her hot chocolate, and insisting she eat regular healthy meals throughout the day.

'What a gem she is,' thought Becky. 'I sure lucked-out when I found her to help me out!'

Chapter 13

In mid-January, Dan and his partner John Knight were at a crime scene where they were investigating to see whether the man had committed suicide or had been killed by another person. There was no suicide note, but there was also no chair or device the man could have stood on to put the noose around his neck. His feet were two feet off the ground, so they couldn't see how he had killed himself.

After the photographer had taken the necessary photos, Dan and John held the body while a uniformed policeman stood on a chair and cut the rope. Dan noticed that John was wincing as he held the man.

'Are you hurting somewhere?' Dan asked quietly.

'Yeah, I've been having problems with my left shoulder and it's even affecting my writing because I'm left-handed.'

'Sounds like it's time to see what's going on,' suggested Dan.

'Yes, I have an appointment with my GP this afternoon.'

'Good. Let me know what he says.'

That afternoon John saw his GP who ordered X-rays. After he examined the X-rays, he recommended that John begin having regular physiotherapy at a sports clinic for his damaged shoulder rotator cuff.

'If the physiotherapy doesn't work, we can consider having cortisone shots, but I want you to try the physio first,' his doctor said.

John went to physiotherapy three times a week for two weeks. One day his physiotherapist watched as he did his shoulder exercises and noticed that nerves in his upper arm were twitching. 'How long has this been happening?' he asked.

'My muscles started twitching a few days ago, especially when I'm flexing it or using it to carry something heavy. I even feel less strength in that arm this week.'

The physiotherapist looked worried, but left John to do his final set of exercises. In the meantime, he went across the hall at the medical centre and had a talk with his brother who was a neurologist. 'I think one of my patients needs to see you,' he said. 'Would you be able to fit him in today?' he asked.

The physiotherapist explained why he wanted him tested before he did more physiotherapy. His brother agreed that he should see him as soon as possible. He checked with his receptionist and learned that his next patient had not arrived yet, so he agreed to see John.

The physiotherapist returned to where John was doing his exercises and told him to stop the set he was doing. He explained that he wanted him to see a specialist who was just across the hall. He also explained that it was his brother and he had been able to fit him in right away.

'Shall I change out of my exercise gear?' John asked.

'No, go as you are, but take your street wear with you,' he replied.

John was curious why the physiotherapist wanted him to see a neurologist, but surmised that the twitching in his arm, might be because of a neurological problem.

'Hello Dr. Baker. Your brother suggested that you might be able to help me with the arm twitching I'm having.'

'Yes, I hope I can.' He examined John, then explained the two tests he would like to conduct.

'What do the tests tell you?' John asked.

'They will show me how the nerves in your body are working,' he explained.

The first test he did was the nerve conduction studies (NCS) that analysed John's nerve function by electrically stimulating his nerves. The machine printed out a recording of his muscle reactions. He examined the printout and nodded his head.

Next, he did an electromyography (EMG) test that consisted of inserting a needle electrode into various muscles to measure their electrical activity. It was a bit painful but not overwhelming.

At the end of the test, Dr. Baker examined those printouts and sadly said, 'I was afraid of this.'

John looked up very concerned at that comment. 'What's wrong with me?' he asked.

'I'm about ninety-five percent sure that you have amyotrophic lateral sclerosis better known as ALS' he replied.

'What's ALS?' John asked. He'd never heard of it.

'There are two other names that are given to it. One you might have heard of – Lou Gehrig's Disease.' John's eyes widened when he heard that name. He knew that the disease was fatal.

Dr. Baker continued, 'And in other parts of the world the disease is known as motor neuron disease MND.'

'What will happen to me if I do have the disease?' John asked. His heart was thumping so hard he thought he was going to pass out. 'Was he going to die?' he wondered.

'It's a terrible disease,' the doctor admitted. 'The neurones in your body – become progressively faulty over time. Neurones control the muscles that allow you to eat, speak, dance, walk, swallow and breathe. Many people can live for a long time with MND, but the average life expectancy is two to three years after diagnosis,' he said sadly.

'Eventually you might need a food tube because you'll lose the ability to swallow. A gastrostomy is a medical procedure during which a permanent tube is placed into the stomach through the abdominal wall. This tube can be used for liquid food and fluids. And towards the end, you might also require a respirator to breathe.'

101

'Oh my God,' John moaned as tears began falling down his cheeks.

Dr. Baker patted his shoulder and said, 'I hate that I'm the one to give you this terrible news, but it's better that you know sooner rather than later.'

'How fast will the disease progress,' John asked when he was able to control his sobbing.

'Every patient is different. There have been some who live for ten years – but the average is two or three years. We won't know until we're able to monitor your progress.'

'Is there anything I can do to counteract the disease?' John asked hopefully. He didn't want to leave his family and was ready to fight till the last breath.

'Unfortunately, it's one of the diseases we haven't been able to cure, but there is a medication that can slow down the process in some patients. I'll give you a prescription for that medication,' he said as he wrote out a prescription.

'Here's a brochure that explains the disease more fully,' he said as he led John to the door of his office.

John was in shock. He had intended to go back to work after his physiotherapy session, but he couldn't face anyone, but knew he had to talk to someone. He phoned Dan on his personal mobile phone. 'Where are you Dan?' he asked.

'I'm on my way back to the office. I'll see you there,' he replied.

'Is there any chance we can meet for coffee before you go to the office?' he pleaded.

Dan could hear that John was upset about something, so suggested they meet at their favourite coffee shop. Dan arrived a few minutes before John and was shocked to see how white and shaky John appeared. He knew John had an appointment that day with his physiotherapist and wondered what had happened.

John sobbed as he told Dan the news. He was glad they were in a booth and others could not see him. 'I'm only forty-seven now and it looks as if I won't even make it to fifty!'

'Oh John, I'm so sorry. I don't know anything about that disease. Can you tell me more about it? He asked.

John handed him the brochure the doctor had given him. As Dan read the information, he too started looking pale. His poor partner was facing a horrible death from one of the cruellest diseases known to man. The brochure said:

Motor Neuron Disease (MND also known as amyotrophic lateral sclerosis ALS and Lou Gehrig's disease) is a progressive degenerative disease that affects muscular function. Its hallmark is the selective death of motor neurons in the brain and spinal cord, which leads to paralysis of voluntary muscles.

Initial symptoms can be:

- Muscle aches, cramps, twitching.
- Clumsiness, stumbling due to weakness of the leg muscles.
- Difficulty holding objects due to weakness of the hand muscles.
- Weakness or changes in hands, arms, legs and voice.
- Slurring of speech.
- Swallowing difficulties due to weakness of the tongue and throat muscles.
- Fatigue.
- Muscle wasting, weight loss.
- Emotional problems.
- Cognitive change.
- The bladder is not usually directly affected by MND; however, some people experience changes to bladder control.

- Constipation can occur, especially when people become less mobile or must change their diet due to swallowing difficulties.

In the past, it was thought that MND only affected the nerve cells controlling the muscles that enable us to move, speak, breathe and swallow. However, approximately fifty percent of people with MND may experience some change in cognition, language, behaviour and personality. When cognitive and behaviour changes occur in MND, it is because there have been changes in specific areas of the brain called the frontal and temporal lobes. Most people experience relatively mild changes. However, a small proportion (five to fifteen percent) will show more significant changes and will receive a diagnosis of 'motor neurone disease with frontotemporal dementia' or MND/FTD. Often the symptoms of dementia precede the motor symptoms, sometimes by several years.

At first, the symptoms can be mild and generally reveal themselves with a loss of muscle function in the hands or feet. Then, the degeneration of nerves leads to the loss of muscle function throughout the entire body. Its progression can be slow or rapid and varies significantly from person to person. Lung capacity can be compromised which means breathing becomes difficult and even swallowing can be affected. Most people with MND retain all senses (sight, hearing, taste, smell, touch) their intellect and memory.

Riluzole is the only approved therapy for MND. It directly or indirectly blocks molecules in the spinal cord called glutamate receptors. Blocking these receptors seems to slow motor neuron loss that leads to paralysis. However, there are many types of glutamate receptors in the spinal cord and it is not yet known which of these are important for MND progression.

There is no known cause(s) or cure for MND. Statistics illustrate how nebulous our knowledge of the disease is: while five to ten percent of cases are familial the other ninety to ninety-five percent are a mystery. While MND does take several forms, ALS is the most common.

At the diagnostic stage, most people have little or no prior knowledge of MND and are devastated to find they have a fatal disease without a cause or treatment. As the disease process advances, patients become reliant on others for assistance with activities of daily living. This can be physically and emotionally demanding for families and carers and patients can experience feelings of guilt, frustration and hopelessness. Many require anti-depressive medication to help them cope with the illness.

Dan looked up at John. 'This is awful. Did the doctor say you could continue to work?'

'He said I could continue to do anything I want to, but to realize that my health will start diminishing sooner or later. I'd like to continue working as long as I can, but I'll have to let them know what's happening to me. Today, though, all I want to do is go home and be with my family. Can you tell my boss that I won't be in for the rest of the day? And will you come with me tomorrow when I speak to our commanding officer?'

'Of course I will. I won't tell them anything this afternoon though, just that you needed the afternoon off.'

John's coworkers were very supportive of him and each of them said that if he needed help in any way, he was to ask. Dan began picking him up in the morning and was their driver when they went on-site to crime scenes.

John was able to work for six weeks, but by then he'd begun stumbling when he walked and started slurring his words when he spoke. It was also an effort to hold a coffee cup. He talked to his commanding officer about his deterioration and was placed on sick leave. He was thankful that his company had a long-term disability policy, so knew he would still be receiving most of his salary.

His wife Sue bought him a tilt-chair, so he could get in and out of the chair, and had Dan install a railing along the hallway for him to hang onto when he went to the bathroom. The bathroom seat had been raised and there were handles on the wall beside the toilet that he could use to raise and lower himself. Sue had asked for and been given a leave of absence from her advertising firm. However, as John's health deteriorated, she realized that she was not strong enough to continue helping him. Although he had lost an alarming amount of weight, he was a tall man and was still too heavy for her to manage.

The ALS Society in Edmonton recommended that they hire a male carer and they were able to find an excellent one for them. He helped John five days a week. The Society also provided him with a wheelchair.

Sue was then able to return to work because they really needed her salary.

On John's birthday, his co-workers came to his home, bundled him up and carried him out to one of their cars.

'Where are we going? he mumbled.

'We're taking you to your favourite restaurant and want you to order anything you want.' Dan said.

John asked for garlic prawns and enjoyed his meal and even got tipsy on the wine. Everyone in the group knew that it wouldn't be long until he would require a food tube. His carer had come with him to help him if he choked on any food. They were all pleased to see that he didn't choke during the meal, and he had a big smile on his face when they took him home.

Six months after John had been diagnosed, the ALS Society did an assessment of his health and recommended that he have a hospital bed placed in his living room. They also installed a sling that could take him from the bed and hoist him over to place him into his tilt chair. A month later, he had a food tube put into his stomach because he couldn't swallow properly. By this time people had to pay close attention to him when he talked, because his speech was heavily affected.

Their daughter, Cindy was just eleven, but she was a great help to her dad, and even their dog Buddy seemed to know that he was ill and stayed by his side as much as he could.

Sue had bought a computer that had a big keyboard and John was able to slowly type messages. The computer also had a device that would speak for him. All he had to do was to highlight what he had printed, and it would say the words.

One time when Dan came to see him, John asked his carer to leave the room because he needed to talk to Dan about something private. Dan looked questioningly at John, wondering what he wanted to discuss.

'Thanks for your regular visits Dan. You're the only one I can really talk to about this horrible disease. I just wish I still had my revolver, because I'm ready to end it all. I hate what's happened to me – look at me,' he said as he gestured with his eyes at his body that was slowly but surely becoming paralyzed. By this time, he was sobbing openly, and Dan came over to his tilt-chair and tried to comfort him.

'I can't even imagine how awful it is for you and wish there was something that we could do to help you. I think it's time that you agreed to take the tranquilizers your doctor wants you to have. I know you're not in pain, and I'm thankful for that, but your emotional status must be very bad,' he said as he patted his shoulder.

John nodded and just knowing that Dan was aware of his mental anguish was enough. During the day he tried to keep his spirits up for Sue and Cindy, but at night he cried many tears of anguish at his condition. Dan was sorry that he had to go back to work and went into the kitchen to talk to John's carer. 'He's very depressed and needs all the help he can get to handle the mental stress of his illness. I've suggested to him that he take the tranquilizers he's been refusing to take. He needs one today, but I would keep them away from him, because I think he's becoming suicidal. Please don't say anything to Sue. He doesn't want her to know he's this depressed.'

As he left, Dan returned to say goodbye to John. He told him that he should be honest when he was with his carer, that he would be able to understand how he was feeling. Dan knew that the carer's sister had died of motor neuron disease and that's why he specialized in caring for those kinds of patients.

John nodded his head, and Dan left for work.

Sue had installed a baby monitor, so she could hear him if he stirred during the night. She was aware of how often he cried during the night, but thought it was best to not let him know that she knew.

John's co-workers made regular visits and they often played a form of scrabble. John would type out the word he wanted on the computer. So, everyone did their best to keep his spirits up.

Eight months after being diagnosed, it became necessary that John be moved to a palliative care hostel. By now, he could move very few parts of his body, and he could not speak much at all. His hands were useless, so he couldn't even type words on the computer. To overcome this, Sue devised a sign board that had three lines with the alphabet on it. If John wanted to say something, she took the board and pointed to one of the lines. If the letter he wanted was on that line, he blinked once – if it wasn't, he would blink twice. Once he chose the line, she would say the letter and he would blink again. He soon became good at this form of communication and Sue was glad that he could do so.

One word he had her help him with was the word 'funeral.' Both knew that it wouldn't be long now until he died. It had only been one year since he'd been diagnosed, so his disease had fast-tracked through his system. They discussed the funeral and Sue said the words she needed to say, 'John, are you afraid to die?'

He blinked once, and a tear slid down his cheek.

'Are you afraid that you might choke to death?'

He blinked once again.

Sue quickly reassured him, 'I want you to know that I've spoken with the nurses and they have assured me that they won't let that happen.'

He blinked again.

Sue had been advised by John's doctor, that many of his patients needed to receive permission to die. Sue felt this was the time to give him that permission. 'John, you've fought long and hard against this disease, but I think it's time for you to let go. The nurses have said that if you stop fighting and let yourself go – that it will happen – that you'll probably slip away peacefully in your sleep.'

As she left him that afternoon, she kissed him on the cheek and said the same words she'd been saying to him when she left him, 'Bye John – remember that Cindy and I love you.'

The next morning at ten after five, a nurse from the hospital phoned to tell her that John had died peacefully during the night. He had lived one short year from the time he'd been diagnosed.

It seemed that the entire Edmonton police force including several members of K Division of the RCMP were at his funeral. Sue could see how well liked he'd been with his co-workers and was touched that they had come. She was glad they'd taken out mortgage insurance and when John died, the remainder of the mortgage on their home was paid off. John had a small life insurance policy which helped as well, so financially, the family would do all right.

Chapter 14

The phone rang and when Becky answered it, learned that it was Brenda. 'Are you ready to look at matron of honour dresses?'

'When do you want to look?' Becky queried.

'I'm available today and tomorrow; whenever's best for you,' said Brenda.

'I've just finished editing a book, so am between jobs myself, so today would be fine,' Becky agreed.

'Okay, can I pick you up say at one o'clock?'

'That will be fine. Irma will be here, so she can keep an eye on Mike for me,' she confirmed.

'See you then.'

Knowing that Becky was supposed to take it easy, Brenda had researched on-line and had personally looked at several dresses for Becky in the shops. Becky's favourite colours were peach and turquoise, so she had the two fashion outlets put aside several outfits she thought might do the job. Becky was definitely showing her pregnant status, so she used the expertise of the fashion specialists to suggest the best outfits for Becky.

Becky was amazed at how beautiful all the outfits were. She would have been happy with any of them. She had difficulty choosing her favourite. It didn't take long and within two hours, she'd purchased the dress, been fitted with shoes that had a tiny but cute heel on them.

They both stopped for coffee at a nearby cafe. Brenda could see how tired Becky was, and vowed that she would ensure that the wedding day itself would be a relaxing one for her.

When the big day came on Valentine's day, Dan drove Becky to Brenda's home. Brenda had arranged a special treat for

Becky. She had asked a masseuse to come to her home to give Becky a relaxing massage. She was an expert in dealing with pregnant women. While Becky was having her massage, Brenda had her hair styled. When Becky was finished with the massage, she was so relaxed and mellow that she nearly dozed while she was having her hair done.

Soon it was time for the bride and matron of honour to get dressed. Brenda had been 'over the moon' because her mother agreed to come to the wedding, and she was there to have her hair done as well and help the bride and matron of honour get dressed. They both looked radiant and beautiful when they were finished.

The hairdresser added the small flowers they'd both chosen to put in their hair. There was a knock at the door, and her father announced through it that the limo was there to take them to the church. Brenda wondered how it would go. Her mother was in the room with her, and her father was on the other side of the door. 'Would they make a fuss, or act like adults?' she wondered.

Brenda opened the door and her father stood back in wonder at the beautiful bride standing before him, then he gently leaned forward and gave her a kiss on her cheek. 'You look absolutely beautiful,' he expounded. Then he looked over her shoulder and saw his ex-wife, then added, 'I'm so glad you're here. It's going to be a lovely day for a wedding.'

Brenda's mother blushed, then she also gave him a kiss on the cheek, 'Yes it's their day and we'll make it a good one.'

The wedding party all gave a sigh of relief. There were two limos outside, one for the bride and her father and a second one for the matron of honour and the mother of the bride.

The wedding was simple and beautiful, but by the time the bride and groom did the wedding waltz, Dan could see that Becky was fading. He took her arm, then went over to the bride and groom and made their apologies, 'I think we should go,' he said nodding towards Becky. The couple could see how tired Becky was and quickly said their goodbyes to them. 'I'm sorry I didn't realize sooner how tired you are. Yes, please go home and rest. Thanks so much for being my matron of honour.'

Becky and Dan went home, and he tucked a tired matron of honour into bed. She was asleep as soon as he turned out the light.

Chapter 15

One evening just before the news came on, Dan turned down the sound and said to Becky, 'There's going to be something on the TV about the trial I testified at today. Now that everyone will know about the crime and the criminal, I'd like to tell you more about it. Do you remember the night about six months ago when we were up most of the night because Mike was coughing so hard?' he asked as he turned towards her.

'I sure do. He had that cough for three nights. I hardly got any sleep.'

'Do you also remember that I was called out during one of those nights to investigate an attempted murder?'

'Yes, I do, because we'd both been awake with Mike that night.'

'Well, it certainly was an interesting case. A woman had phoned the emergency number and had calmly spoken with one of our officers. He told me that she said, 'My name is Mabel Fisher. I need the police to come here right away. A man came into my home and tried to kill me, but I was able to disable him. But you'd better come right away because he might wake up and I'll have to use my weapon on him again.'

'The officer got her details and said the police would be there right away. That's when he dispatched a police car and phoned me. We both got there at the same time, and when I knocked on the door was surprised to have an old woman open the door. She invited us in. I asked her who she was and where the man was, and she pointed to a room down the hallway where the lights were on. 'The scumbag's in there,' she said as she pointed the way.

'I drew my gun, and she said, 'Oh, you won't need that. I bashed him a good one and he probably won't wake up for a while.'

'I remember kind of laughing inside thinking that this frail older woman had taken on an intruder. She'd been sitting calmly at her dining room table sipping a cup of tea (at least I assumed it was tea) when I arrived. When I got to the bedroom, I saw a man lying on his side beside the bed, not far from the doorway to the bedroom. I saw that he had packing tape around his wrists that were secured behind his body and noted that the same kind of tape was securing his ankles. He was bleeding quite profusely from a head wound, and I noted that there was a towel under his head.

I leaned over to see if he was breathing and felt his neck to get a pulse and was glad to see that he was still alive. I straightened up and glanced at the bed. There sticking out of the covers was a knife and I wondered if someone was under those covers. Mabel was standing right behind me by this time and said, 'He thought I was under those covers, but I fooled him.'

There was another knock at the front door, and she let the paramedics into her home. I stood back as they examined the man. They asked if they could take the tape off his wrists and I said to go ahead, but to leave the tape on his ankles. I'd checked to ensure that the tape was not shutting off the circulation. They placed him on his back, took his vital signs and put a dressing on his head wound. They then asked permission to put him on a gurney that was waiting for him in the living room. They did so, and I asked the uniformed officer to cuff his hand to the gurney and to accompany him to the hospital. He was to stay with him until he was relieved.'

'I then called our office to alert them to the fact that we had an injured prisoner who would need twenty-four-hour surveillance until he was released from the hospital. I warned them that he had attempted to murder a woman and was a dangerous person.'

'After photographing the scene, I carefully bagged the knife and bloody towel and went back to the dining room. I told

Mabel that I needed to fill in a report. She agreed and after giving details of her name, address ,and age etc. I was amazed when she told me her age, 'I was seventy-five two weeks ago,' she said proudly.

By this time, Becky was chuckling as she pictured the scene and then encouraged him to continue.

'Then I asked her what had happened. She said that as usual she'd gone to the bathroom during the night about two o'clock. It was about fifteen minutes later that she heard a floor creak in the kitchen and immediately thought it was her little dog going to his doggie-door but remembered that he was staying overnight at the vets because of a bad cough he'd developed. Then she heard another sound she recognized as someone walking through her kitchen. She told me she slipped out of bed and arranged her pillows to look as if she was still in bed, then picked up a weapon and backed into the alcove that led off her bedroom into a walk-in closet and bathroom.'

'She said she was surprised at how well she could see in the dark and gave credit to the fact that she'd just had cataract operations on both eyes a month ago. She went on to say that the man hesitated at the door and turned left towards the bed then made a slicing motion down onto the bed. It was when he straightened up from doing this that she 'whacked' him with her weapon.'

'I asked her to describe her weapon and she rose from the dining room chair, went to the kitchen and returned with her 'weapon.' Do you know what it was?' he asked with a chuckle.

'A baseball bat?' she replied with a smile.

'Nope; it was a meat tenderizer – you know those things that look like a hammer with a flat area on one side and a kind of bumpy area on the other. I could see from the blood on the implement that she'd hit him with the flat side and winced when I thought of the injury she would have inflicted if she'd used the other side. So, I had another weapon to confiscate. In the meantime, by the way, she'd made me a cup of tea and we were both sitting calmly at the dining room table sipping tea at three o'clock in the morning.'

'She continued telling her story. She said she was glad she was moving away from the place because of the break-in, and that she wouldn't have had the packing tape as handy as it was if she hadn't been packing boxes the day before. She told me how hard it was to shift him onto his side, so she could tape his hands and feet together. She kind of looked after his welfare though, because she said she made sure that she put him into the recovery position – that she didn't want him to die even though he was a scumbag.' By now both he and Becky were laughing openly.

'How did the trial go today?' Becky asked as she recovered.

'I think you'll find out by watching the news. It's just coming on now.'

The news announced that a man had been sentenced to seven years in jail for attempting to murder a seventy-five-year-old woman in her home. The feisty woman was able to disable him with a meat tenderizer. At this point they flashed a scene where Mabel was leaving the court house with a big smile on her face.

'I'm sure most people watching this broadcast are amazed at the woman. I had to warn her that there would be a media frenzy after the trial, but she calmly said, 'Remember, I'm not going to be living there any more! They'll have no idea where I live because I now have an unlisted number and only my close friends and the police know it.'

'I felt it was a pleasure to meet someone of her calibre. It turns out she used to be a fitness trainer and still goes to the gym twice a week, competes in ping-pong tournaments and participated last year in the Multiple Sclerosis walk,' Dan concluded.

Chapter 16

In mid-March, Shirley Roberts phoned Becky. She was very excited as she said, 'I can't believe how many of my books have been sold! The book tour has been fantastic. I've seen parts of Canada that I've never seen before. It's been so exciting,' she finished, taking a breath.

Becky chuckled, 'Yes it's quite an experience isn't it. I'll bet you didn't expect to be on Canada AM and all the other special television programs, did you?'

'It's amazing to see in person the people you see on the news every night. The radio shows have been great too. I was on one that was a call-in show and so many women called in to say how similar their stories were to mine, but some of them were still with their partners. I think some of them might now have the courage to leave their battering spouses and partners.'

'There was one lady who called in to say she was worried about her son. Her husband had hit him three times over the bottom with his belt the night before and the child could not sit down that day. I asked her if she wanted my advice, and she said yes. I told her that she should take coloured photos of her son's injuries, take him to a doctor, get the doctor to put in writing the injuries her son had received, then she should go to the police and file an assault and child abuse charge against her husband. I hope she does it. Anyway, I feel that I'm doing something worth-while and will end up receiving lots of royalties to boot.'

'How did the newspaper interviews go?' Becky asked.

'They went very well. In fact, one of them suggested that I write a regular column where people can write in with problems they're facing in their relationships and I'll answer them in the column. Life couldn't get much better!'

'Just wait till the paperback book comes out in a few months. By then you'll be a household name and the books should jump off the shelves. Jim Stevens has said I might be the one to do that book tour. We'll hit most of the same media people but will possibly add some international media like the Oprah Show.' Becky explained.

'Wow, I didn't think my book would go outside Canada. That would be great if it went international.'

'I'm sure Jim is negotiating with world-wide publishers and some of them would publish your book in their language.'

'How does that work? Will we have to arrange for the translations?'

'No, the foreign language publishers will take the English version and translate it into their language. They'll then release it world-wide in that language.' Becky explained. 'Jim will present you with a contract from each of the publishers explaining the agreement – advance on royalties, and the percentage of royalties you will receive. Most contracts have a five- to seven-year span. After that time, they have the option of renewing the contract, and by this time your percentage of royalties will normally be higher.'

'It's quite complicated, isn't it?' Shirley asked.

'Yes, but you're with one of the best publishers to do it. And with so many people buying books they can read on their Kindle and other tablets; your eBooks should also sell very well. The foreign publishers might include that in their contracts as well, so you would be receiving royalties from foreign eBooks as well.'

'Wow! I had no idea what I was getting into when I gave my manuscript to my cover-designer friend!' she exclaimed.

'Just wait! You haven't even spoken with Jim about this, but we might make a movie out of your book, so it doesn't stop there – it goes on and on!' she explained.

'I had no idea that my book could be made into a movie. Do you really think it's that good?'

'Yes, I do, in fact I was the one who suggested it to Jim. However, we won't approach the movie companies until after your paperback edition comes out. You'll likely sell far more of those editions, which will be a selling point to get the film-makers interested.'

'You're overwhelming me with all of this. I thought I was only going to write a little book and get it published but look what's happening with it! I can't get over it!' she exclaimed.

'So, that's an incentive for you to write another book. Have you given much thought to that idea?' Becky encouraged.

'As a matter of fact, I've drafted an outline for my next book. It will talk about my transition from being a battered wife, to going back to work, back to dating, being a single mom, and eventually starting my own company and travelling around the globe. I think the last part will be a book in itself. I'll have to see how the second one goes.'

'I'm glad to hear that you're thinking along those lines. I've been told by other writers that if you do a few pages of your book every day, it will soon be written. Sometimes you will get on a 'roll' and will do several chapters, but there will also be other days when you'll have writer's block.'

'I ran into that even writing the outline. I couldn't think of enough things to put in the book.' Shirley agreed.

'Don't worry about those days, just do something else, and the ideas will come to you as you're diverted elsewhere. Trust me on this. I've talked to so many writers who battle writer's block, that I've learned that it's a temporary thing.

Chapter 17

Becky was now at the stage where she had to see her doctor every week. He kept an eye on her developing baby and everything was going well. Her last pregnancy had ended in having a stillborn child after many hours in labour. Her water had broken when she was only seven months pregnant, so that was the time the doctor paid much more attention to her welfare. The first of April came and went, and she passed the seven-month milestone. She felt almost as if she were holding her breath. She was doing very little at home except some pre-natal exercises approved by her doctor and taking a few walks around the block with another member of her family.

She stopped picking Mike up and had to explain to him why she had to do that. One day he put his head to the side, and looking up at her, he said, 'Mommy, do you know that you're getting fat?'

Becky laughed and replied, 'Do you know why I'm getting fat?'

'You're eating too much?' he suggested.

Becky laughed again. 'No, mommy has a baby in her tummy. Do you want to feel it kick?'

He looked in wonder at her, not understanding how a baby could kick when he was inside his mother.

Becky sat down and took his little hand and placed it on her tummy. The baby cooperated and did several big kicks. His eyes grew round, and he put his head gently on her tummy.

'Why are you doing that?' Becky asked.

'I was wondering if the baby was saying anything,' he explained.

'You're such a little dear,' Becky said as she ruffled his hair. 'The baby won't be able to breathe and talk till it's born?'

'When will it be born?' he asked.

Becky took him to a wall calendar and showed him when the baby was due. 'The baby will be born about this time. If you want, I will circle that day and you can cross off the days until then. Would you like to do that?'

He nodded his head and went to his room to get a crayon. He circled the date the baby was due and put an X on the calendar to show what today was.

'Every night before you go to bed, you can put another X on the calendar.' Becky explained.

'Is the baby a boy or a girl?' he asked.

'We won't know until the baby is born. What would you like it to be – a boy or a girl?' she asked.

He thought for a minute. Well, I have one brother and one sister, so I guess it doesn't really matter does it?' he said intelligently.

Becky was glad that it wasn't an important issue with Mike.

Becky had told Jim Stevens that she didn't want to do any more editing until a bit after the baby was born but found herself with time on her hands. For many years now, she'd contemplated writing a book herself, but never seemed to have the time to do it with her job and growing family. 'Maybe now's the time to do it,' she thought.

She went to her computer and did what she told her authors to do – she sketched out what she wanted the book to be about. She decided that what she wanted to do was to write about what had happened in her life, but in a fictional way. Things that happened to her, she could embellish and make more interesting, and possibly add extra things to the book that didn't really happen but might have happened to someone she knew.

She was pleased when she finished sketching out what she wanted to write about. That evening, she told Dan what she had been doing that day.

'That sounds like a good idea. Will I learn things about you that I didn't know?' he queried with a smile?

'Oh, you never know!' she teased. 'I have to tell you, that I will be adding things that didn't really happen, so you'll never know what did or didn't happen in my former life.'

'You've got me intrigued. Will I be able to read it when it's done? Before you give it to Jim to have it edited?' he questioned.

'I promise that you'll be the first one to read it. I'll wait until it's completed though, because I'll likely add and subtract things or move things around as I go.'

'I think it's a good idea, but I don't want you sitting in front of the computer for more than an hour at a time. You'll need to get up more often now with so much pressure on your spine. I don't want you getting clots in your legs from sitting too long,' he admonished.

'I promise,' she said holding up her hand in a swearing motion.

'I'll be talking to Irma and will have her monitor if you've been being a good girl,' he threatened.

'Okay boss. I'll be a good girl,' she said with a laugh.

She made good progress with the book for the next two weeks and took the required breaks as she promised.

Dan had gone to work, Sandy had gone to school, and Irma had arrived for the day when Becky realized that her water had broken. She was soaked and there was a big puddle on the bathroom floor. She was going to bend down to clean up the mess when she realized that this would be a 'no-no' so called to Irma to help her.

Irma had been coached by Dan and had even talked with Becky's doctor about what she was to do if Becky went into early labour. She helped Becky change out of her soiled clothing, washed her down and got her into a comfortable pair of sweat pants with a clean towel placed to catch any further water seepage. She called Becky's doctor who said he would send an ambulance to get Becky.

In the meantime, Irma wiped up the spill, checked the little bag Becky had packed for her hospital stay, called Mary next door to see if she could look after Mike, phoned Dan and told him the news, and accompanied Becky in the ambulance to the hospital.

Becky's doctor was already at the hospital when she arrived. He'd been there delivering a baby, so Becky didn't have to wait to see him. He examined her and asked her whether she'd felt any contractions.

''No; so far I haven't, but last time it was several hours after the water broke that the contractions began,' she explained.

'Well, I'm going to give you something that I hope will keep you from going into full labour. You're close to being eight months pregnant, so that's a good sign and your baby is a good size, so even if you do go into labour, your baby should be okay.'

Becky was so relieved to hear him say that but burst into tears anyway. 'I so want this baby to live. Please do anything you need to do to make sure it does.'

He patted her hand, left the room and came back with a nurse who administered the medication Nifedipine that could help her from going into full labour.

'This medication is a muscle relaxant that can slow or stop labour. I'll also be giving you a steroid injection and if you haven't delivered within twelve hours, I'll give you another one. The steroid drug will help your baby's lungs to mature. And I'd like you to have an ultrasound, so we can tell the position and size of your baby,' he said. 'I'll request that be done as soon as possible.'

It was then that Dan arrived, and Becky was able to tell him what the doctor was going to do.

'I'm so sorry you've gone into premature labour,' he said sadly, 'but I understand that because you're now in your thirty-fourth week of pregnancy, the baby has a much better chance.'

'Yes, I hope so. They're going to try to stop me from going into full labour. So far, I've had no labour pains, just the normal contractions that I've been feeling the past month.

The nurse returned to the room and said she was going to take Becky for an ultrasound. 'She won't be long,' she said as she whisked the stretcher past the worried husband.

After the ultrasound, they were relieved when her doctor told her that her child was a good size and was in the proper position to be born 'That's a relief,' they both said at once, then smiled at each other.

'I'm putting a foetal doppler on your tummy to listen to your little one's heartbeat,' he said as he installed the device. Soon they were hearing the ping, ping, ping of the baby's heartbeat.

'It's so fast!' Becky exclaimed.

'That's normal,' he confirmed as he left the room.

The nurse asked Becky, 'Did you have any breakfast this morning?'

'No, I didn't. This happened first thing in the morning.'

'Would you like some coffee and toast?' she asked.

'Make that tea and you've got an order.' Becky replied.

She had almost finished her tea and toast when she realized that she felt very cold. 'Dan, could you ask them if I can have another blanket. I'm freezing.'

'Sure,' he said as he left the room to ask for one.

When he and the nurse arrived back in the room, Becky was shaking like a leaf. Even her teeth were chattering.

127

'What's happening?' he asked.

'I'm not sure, but her body could be going into shock from the early delivery, or it could be infection. I'll get the doctor,' she said as she placed the warmed blanket over Becky.

Within minutes, Becky stopped shaking and her breathing returned to normal. Both looked at the foetal doppler and saw that the baby's heartbeat was going ninety miles per hour.

The nurse returned, and they questioned her about the baby's heartbeat.

'The baby might have felt the panic its mother felt. Hopefully the heartbeat will settle down soon.'

The doctor came into the room and examined Becky and listened with his stethoscope to the baby's heartbeat.

'What's happening doctor?' Dan asked.

'I'm not sure, but I think Becky could have picked up an infection. This can happen when the water breaks. That leaves the mother open to infection and can be quite serious. I'll take a swab of her vagina and have it tested right away,' he promised.

The nurse left and came back with a swab, and then took it directly to pathology. The results that she did indeed have an infection were back very soon, and Becky was put on antibiotics.

She and Dan were relieved, and Becky felt much better. They watched television for a while, but Becky again felt very cold. 'I'm freezing again Dan. I'll need another blanket,' she said worriedly.

Dan immediately went to ask for a warm blanket. Becky looked apprehensively at the foetal doppler and saw that again the baby's heartbeat was again very fast.

Becky's doctor came again arrived said, 'Becky, I think your baby's in trouble. I had hoped this wouldn't happen, but I think we'd better do a caesarean section. Would you agree to that?'

'Anything. Just don't let my baby die!' she wailed.

'I'll set it up,' he said as he left the room.

Dan kissed her, knowing how upset she must be. He was almost in tears himself. How could this be happening to his wife and unborn child?

Almost too soon, Becky was whisked into the operating room, given an epidural and screens were placed between her and her mid-section. They also gave Becky some medication to help her anxiety. She felt nothing and was surprised at how soon she heard a baby wailing and knew that her child had been born.

'It's a little girl,' he announced. 'Just let us clean her up and weigh her, and we'll let you see her.'

'Is she all right?' Becky asked wondering if the child was physically okay.

'She's a lovely baby with all her fingers and toes,' smiled the nurse.

'She's two point four kilograms, or in the old measure, five pounds, three ounces so she's a good size. However, because she's early we'll be taking her to the neonatal unit, so we can monitor her progress. But first, here's your lovely daughter,' he said as he placed her on Becky's chest.

'Could you please hold her up a bit, so I can see her better?' she asked.

He did so, and she could see what a lovely child she was.

Becky was taken back to her room and met an excited Dan. 'Well done sweetheart. The nurse told me we have a lovely little girl and that I can see her in a couple of minutes in the neonatal unit. I'll be back soon,' he promised.

An hour later, the nurse came in with a wheelchair and asked Becky if she wanted to have another look at her baby. She and Dan stood outside the glass of the neonatal unit marvelling at the little girl in the cot that had 'Jeffries Baby' on the cot. Dan took a couple of pictures with his mobile phone.

'I'll be able to show these to Sandy and Mike tonight.' Their little girl was so tiny and perfect he didn't know what to say. Becky noticed the tears running down his cheeks and knew what a special day it was for her family.

'What are we going to call her?' Dan asked.

'I'd like to call her Victoria – Vicki for short. That was my grandmother's name, and I loved her dearly.' Becky suggested.

'I like that too. Can we make her middle name Deanna after my aunt in Australia?' he asked.

'That would be a good combination – Victoria Deanna Jeffries. It has a ring to it doesn't it, and seems to fit.'

They both agreed to that name being put on her birth certificate.

Because she'd had a caesarean and was still fighting her infection, Becky was kept in the hospital for four days but was not allowed to hold her baby. They had allowed Sandy and Mike to come up to see her and their new sister, but they could only stay for a short time. Mike couldn't believe that the little baby in the cot was his new sister.

'Mom, how come she came so early? I still have lots of days on the calendar to cross off,' he said with a sideways look.

'Well, I guess she just couldn't wait to meet her brother,' Becky made light of it.

'When can we take her home?' he asked as he looked up at his dad.

'Well, she might be in for a few more days than Mom is, but she should be home soon.' Dan explained.

Becky was not able to breastfeed Vicki because of her infection but was glad that there were other mothers who were kind enough to donate breast milk. Becky had been shown how to use a breast pump, so she would keep her milk coming, but the milk had to be destroyed because of her infection. She couldn't wait till the infection was finally over, so she could hold her child. She'd watched Dan through the glass as he held their little girl. She latched on right away to his finger, just as Sandy had done the day Becky and Shane had adopted her.

On the sixth day after Vicki was born, they were finally given the 'go ahead' to take her home. Becky was able to hold and breastfeed her for the first time and couldn't believe how wonderful it felt to be able to hold her baby and suckle her.

Mike was quite excited when he could sit on the sofa and Becky placed his sister in his arms. 'She's cute,' he said. 'Can I take her for walks in her new stroller?'

'It's still a bit too cool for her to be taken outside for a walk, but you can sit in the back seat and watch her for us when we go for car rides. How would that be?' Becky replied.

'Okay. I'm glad she can have my old car seat, because I'm much too big to use it now,' he said in a boastful way. He felt very grown-up beside his tiny little sister.

Sandy was so pleased that it was a girl. She had fun helping Becky choose little dresses and outfits for her new sister, and Becky often saw her peeking around the corner during the night as she sat in the rocking chair nursing Vicki.

'Just checking to see that someone's feeding her,' was her excuse.

'Back to bed you go sweetheart. You have to go to school tomorrow, and I don't want you to be too tired,' she scolded.

Dan had a bit of trouble adjusting to having a baby cry and found that he too woke up when Vicky gave her hungry cries.

They had a baby monitor in their bedroom, so were able to hear Vicki when she woke up. Mike woke up when Vicki cried the first couple of nights but was soon sleeping through the night again.

Everyone adjusted to the change of having a new baby, and life returned to normal. Irma still came five days a week while Becky was recovering from her caesarean, but they soon found that Becky could manage with her coming just three days a week as she did before. Becky often saw her peering into Vicki's little bed with wonderment in her eyes. She loved little Vicki and was constantly knitting her little sweaters and booties, and she bought her a tiny pair of soft leather booties.

Becky had decided not to accept any more manuscripts until Vicki was two months old and still intended to work from home because it was so much easier for her to do. During that two months, she kept dabbling at her book, and soon had it half finished.

She phoned Jim to tell him that she was ready to edit books again but wanted to still work out of her home.

Jim replied, 'How are you and your little one doing?'

'We're doing great. She's such a good baby. She only wakes up once during the night and goes right back to sleep after her feed. So yes, things are great,' she replied honesty.

'Good to hear that. I'm going to ask you something and feel free to say no if you can't do it. Shirley Roberts's book is about to be released in paperback and eBook formats, so we will be arranging for another book tour. This one will be more extensive though and we'll be trying to get her some publicity in the United States as well. I'm wondering if you're up to doing this or is this too soon?' he asked.

'It will be a big promotion, but I already have the details from the launch of her hard cover edition, and I have the necessary US contacts from the book we launched last year. I think I'm up to arranging the book tour, but I don't think I can do the tour itself. The main reason I say that is that if I went on tour with Shirley, I'd have to take Vicki with me because I'm breastfeeding her. I would also need someone to babysit her while I was touring Shirley around. This would obviously cost more because we would be flying all over the country. And secondly, I don't think it's a good idea to expose Vicki to all the ills that can happen to frequent flyers. I hope you don't mind me backing out on you,' she ended sounding worried.

'As I said, I wanted you to say no if you couldn't do it. Why don't we have you set up the interviews and I can get someone else to do the actual book tour?' he suggested.

'That sounds like a good plan to me. When did you plan on having the book tour start and how extensive do you want it to be in Canada?' she queried.

'I think we should plan on doing it in mid-July. The weather will be great at that time, so people will be out and about. As far as the media we should contact, I think we should hit all the spots we did before. In fact, I think we should contact everyone we did last time, even the ones that did not do interviews for the hard cover edition. The more coverage we can get the better.'

'Okay. I'll get busy trying to set it up. Which side of Canada do you want to start on – the Maritime Provinces or British Columbia - and do you want to do the States before or after Canada?'

He thought for a bit then said, 'I think we should start in British Columbia and go eastward, then when we get to the Maritime Provinces, we can then go down to New York and start the US segment going westward.'

'I'll plan on that. How long a tour do you want and what kind of expense account will we have for it?' she asked.

He named a figure, and she was astounded at the amount. 'Wow – this will be some book tour!' she exclaimed.

'Her hard cover edition's sales are phenomenal, and I know that the paperback and eBook editions will do even better, so that will be money well spent.'

'Okay, leave it with me. I'll keep you updated on my progress in getting the tour on-track.'

It was hard slogging and with family interruptions throughout the day she had to work late many evenings.

'Are you sure this isn't too much for you?' Dan asked.

'It is hard slogging I must admit, but there's an end in sight. And besides with the time changes across Canada, it's sometimes better that I'm available to contact others in our evening and sometimes to reach those that are east of us before eight in the morning. I promise you I'll rest a bit during the day – I won't keep at it all day. I'll crash if I do that!' she acknowledged.

Finally, the day came when she was able to send the schedule to Jim and Shirley. When she talked to Shirley she said, 'It will be a full-on tour and you'd better rest up, so you'll be up to the challenge,' Becky warned her.

'I'm so excited about this tour. The last one was great, but I was so self-conscious being on television and radio that I was terribly stressed throughout the tour. This time I think I'll enjoy it more. And the chance to be on programs in the US such as the Ellen DeGeneres Show, the View Show where I'll be interviewed by both Rosie O'Donnell and Whoopi Goldberg is amazing. You've even been able to get me on the Tonight Show and I'll be interviewed by Piers Morgan who hosts the former Larry King Show.'

'It took a little convincing for me to get them to agree to accept a Canadian author, so it's now up to you to go out there full of confidence. By that time in the tour, you'll have been on television throughout Canada, so will be an old hand at it,' she encouraged.

'Thank you so much for doing so much work for me. This will be a great opportunity for me.'

'By the way – how are you doing with your sequel to that book?'

'I can't believe it but this one almost wrote itself. I won't have time to check the grammar and spelling before I start on the tour, but possibly after the tour is over, I can get back to it.'

'I'd be glad to edit it as it is if you would like me to do so. You can always add or move things around after the tour, but at least I can have the opportunity of working with it while you're on tour. What do you say?'

'Okay, just before I go on tour, I'll send a disk copy of the manuscript to you, but please be aware that it will be a first draft.'

'I understand and will take that into account when I edit it.' Becky promised.

Chapter 18

When the manuscript arrived, Becky found the content of the book was as good as Shirley's first one. As expected, there were many grammatical and spelling errors she had to correct and several places where she suggested that an area be explained a bit better, but basically it was as good a book as her first one.

This story was about what happened after Shirley left her battering husband - starting from when she'd moved from Winnipeg to Calgary with her three children. Calgary was booming at that time, and she didn't find it difficult to obtain a job as legal secretary in a law office that specialized in real estate home sales. She soon became bored with the job and realized that she was doing all the work and her boss was raking in the profits. All he had to do was to give her the details of the sale, and she completed all the paperwork.

She'd asked herself, 'Is this all there is?' and decided to set some goals for herself. Her life had become so much better now that she didn't have to live in the same city as her battering husband. The children were settled into their new schools, but still she felt very restless. 'What's next?' she wondered.

Her office had just upgraded to using computers, and she loved working with them and convinced her boss that she needed to take courses, so she understood them better. Soon she was taking computer courses and when her company wouldn't pay for some, she paid for them herself. One of her instructors said she had a real talent for working with computers and encouraged her to take some courses that would enable her to become an electronic engineering technologist. She decided to follow his advice and for the next three years took evening courses. She also changed jobs and worked as a secretary for a medium-sized oil company to learn as much as she could about the oil industry.

Her social life had been pretty sparse and at first she hesitated to accept an invitation to have dinner at another secretary's home. She finally accepted, but soon learned that it was so she could meet a man who was ten years younger than she. Keith was a real character and had a child-like attitude towards life and they talked up a storm during dinner. She learned that he was a salesman and a volunteer for the Calgary Stampede Board in charge of the 'White Hatter' presentations. He explained that when national or foreign dignitaries visited Calgary, he would present them with a white Calgary Stampede hat.

They started dating and had such fun together that they became lovers. He was fabulous with her children and they grew to love him as well.

After graduating from her course, Shirley found that she had problems being accepted as an electronic engineering technologist and was aware that this was happening because she was a woman. She'd been the only woman taking the course and only the tenth woman who had graduated. Finally, in desperation, she applied for and was offered a job at a major pipeline company in Edmonton. She didn't want to leave Keith but knew that she needed to start using her new skills. Keith agreed that she should take the job, and that Edmonton was only three hundred kilometres north of Calgary, so they could still spend weekends together.

They made love that Saturday night, and it wasn't until 'the deed was done' that they both realized that he had not used a condom. She'd warned him that she'd had to go off birth control pills a couple of months before because of their side effects. The doctor wanted her to go three months without them and then he would prescribe a different one.

'Keith, do you realize we didn't use a condom?' she said, full of concern.

'Shit, I was so carried away with the thought that I was going to lose you that I forgot. It would be just our luck that one of my little fellows is saying hello to one of yours right now,' he added, trying to get some humour into the situation.

'Well, with me just starting a new job, the timing couldn't be worse,' she added full of concern.

'I guess we'll just have to wait and see,' he suggested.

The next day Shirley could tell she was ovulating. One of the side effects of being off her birth control pills was that she had mid-month pain at the time she was ovulating. She knew she could be in trouble and was going to phone Keith about it when her phone rang.

'Hi Shirley,' he said sadly.

She could tell something was wrong. 'What's wrong?' she asked.

He was sobbing as he said, 'I've just received a phone call telling me that my mother has died of a massive stroke. She was only fifty-eight!' he exclaimed.

'Oh Keith, I'm so sorry. I guess you'll have to go to Ottawa to arrange her funeral. Will your brother and his wife go with you?' she asked.

'I've just got off the phone from him and we've made airline reservations to leave this afternoon, so I won't be able to see you before I go.'

'That's okay. Phone me when you get there. If there's anything you need me to do at this end, let me know.'

'I will. Bye for now,' he ended sadly.

It wasn't until she got off the phone that she realized she hadn't told him about the possibility she could be pregnant. She mulled over what she should do, and finally talked to a girlfriend she could trust. Her girlfriend told her about a new 'day after pill' that was on the market that Shirley's doctor could prescribe.

First thing the next morning, she phoned her family doctor and made an appointment with her for that day. The doctor gave her the prescription, and a few days later Shirley had a period. So that problem was solved, and she decided that she would not tell Keith anything about it except to let him know that she wasn't pregnant.

Then it was time to start packing and finding a home in Edmonton. She sold her Calgary home very quickly, so knew she'd have to hustle to get another one before the possession date. Her job didn't start for a month, so she had time to settle in.

For two years, her son Peter had been taking courses at the University of Alberta in Calgary and it would be necessary for him to transfer his studies to the Edmonton campus. However, he decided that he didn't want to move to Edmonton and asked whether he could share accommodation with another student. So, it was only Shirley and her daughter that moved to Edmonton. Her middle son, Ron was already working on a pipeline near Whitecourt, about one hundred kilometres north of Edmonton, so both her sons wouldn't be too far away.

Her new job entailed ensuring that the switching on the pipeline kept the oil and gas running smoothly. This occasionally involved travelling to different isolated sites where she would wear the company's coveralls. It was often cold and uncomfortable during these callouts, but she worked with another technician, so they were able to work in tandem correcting any computer problems they faced.

Most of those trips were day trips, but occasionally she had to stay overnight at towns near the relay stations. She found that when she worked in the main office in Edmonton, she was often called upon to help her co-workers with other computer problems, and really enjoyed that part of her job. She enjoyed it so much that she contacted the people at the Northern Alberta Institute of Technology in Edmonton to ask if they needed someone to present computer courses. They hired her immediately, and she offered two-hour courses three evenings a week. The only time she had to re-schedule was when she had to stay out of town overnight.

She and Keith had tried to keep their relationship going, but both were out of town so often that it was sometimes only a few days a month that they were able to get together.

It wasn't long before Shirley realized that her life was mostly work, work, and more work now that she was living in Edmonton. She missed having a social life. Another female worker at her office seemed to have a very active social life. Shirley asked her how she met available men and was surprised to learn that most of her dates were found when she went to a dating service in the city. Shirley bit the bullet, and made an appointment to see the retired lady, Margaret Brown, who ran it, and signed up. She was glad she did because she met some special men through that service. She became quite adept at sussing out men on their first meeting. Most of the time they met after several talks via telephone (there was no e-mail at this time) and after several phone calls where they learned more about each other. The next step was to meet in person for coffee.

Margaret would already have asked the pertinent questions of her applicants such as marital status, age, height, weight, physical condition, education etc. so these areas were known before Shirley met them for coffee. It was during the coffee meetings that she was able to determine whether there was a 'spark' or interest in pursuing the relationship. One out of two or three times, this would be the only time she would meet with men referred to her.

After one meeting, she phoned Margaret and asked to speak with her and cautioned her about the man she'd met that day for coffee. 'There's something 'off' about him. I don't know what it is, but think you need to investigate him further. It might be a good idea to see if he has a criminal record,' she warned.

'What kind of warning bells are you seeing in this man?' Margaret asked showing great interest in what she was hearing. She respected Shirley and knew she would not be making those comments unless she felt they were true.

'I wish I could put my finger on it, but I found myself mentally and physically on alert when I met him. It was something in the way he looked at me – like a predator. I felt threatened by him even though on the surface we did nothing but have small-talk,' Shirley admitted.

'Okay. I usually don't do a police check, but in this case, I think I'd better do so. I don't want one of my female applicants put in danger if he's as bad as your instincts tell you he is,' she promised.

Shirley nodded her head as she said, 'Thanks for doing that. Will you let me know what the police report says?' Margaret promised she would.

Several days later Margaret phoned Shirley and said that she'd been right. The man had a criminal record and had been charged and incarcerated twice for raping women. She added that she'd told the police that he'd registered with her dating service and wondered if he was registered with other dating services. If so, could they warn them that he was dangerous?

'We'll keep an eye on him. Thanks for taking the time to investigate him. He hasn't been out of jail very long so he's probably back doing what he did before.' They promised to put a tail on him and he was apprehended two weeks later when a woman reported that he'd tried to rape her. She'd taken self-defence courses and was able to gouge his eyes and get away from him. Soon he was back in jail.

Margaret asked Shirley whether she would investigate other men she suspected were liars. Even though she had them come to her home for the interview, she didn't trust her instincts when she felt something was wrong. It was an asset that Shirley was willing to meet the men first before they went out on other dates. Shirley and Margaret were able to eliminate two other men who were compulsive liars, and one that was simply a user of women.

Shirley did meet some nice men. One was Joseph Dietrich or as he called himself, 'Joe.' He was tall, thin, and quite athletic. In her conversations with him, Margaret learned that he'd competed in the Winter Olympics as a skier for Austria and had won a bronze medal. Shirley didn't downhill ski, but she did enjoy cross-country skiing and they spent several Saturday afternoons skiing the trails specially set up for cross-country skiers.

On one of her son Peter's weekend visits, Joe taught him how to downhill ski. Later, Peter became a volunteer ski patroller and spent many years enjoying the sport. Shirley and Joe went out to dinner and had quiet evenings at home and eventually became lovers. For some reason they drifted apart and eventually stopped seeing each other.

Shirley was at a breakfast meeting one day when she sat beside a man who was also a specialist in computers. 'Hi, I'm Ernie Larson,' he said introducing himself. Shirley did likewise. She liked his smile and his laughing eyes and felt attracted to him.

After the meeting, he asked her whether he could see her again. During the meeting Shirley had noticed that he wore a wedding ring, and in her book, it was a no-no to date married men. She simply tapped her finger on his wedding ring and said, 'I don't date married men.'

'I keep telling myself that I should take this thing off. My wife and I are separated, but we still live in the same home because of our children. I think it's time I did something to change the situation,' he admitted.

'Well, when you're truly separated and not living with your wife, why don't you phone me?' she suggested.

He agreed, and she waited anxiously to see if he would call her. In the meantime, Shirley went back to Margaret to meet other available men.

The next man she suggested lived in a town not far from Edmonton. His name was Darren McKenzie and he seemed to be a very interesting person. When they met for coffee, Darren told her that in his earlier years, he'd trained as an Air Force pilot. He'd been two weeks away from getting his pilot's licence, when his car was rear-ended by a huge, out-of-control gravel truck. He pointed to his head and said, 'I have a steel plate in my head from the injuries and spent nine months in a coma. They thought I would never wake up from it, but I fooled them all. As expected though, I couldn't be a pilot, and was booted out of the Air Force. I had a long rehabilitation period and became interested in all the things disabled people needed just to get through the day. So, I decided to start a company that supplied wheelchairs, walkers, crutches, tilt chairs, hospital beds, slings to help move paralysed patients, ramps to homes, raised toilet seats, hallway railings and other devices that made a disabled person's life easier.'

Then he said proudly, 'My company took off like a rocket, and I'm still able to help many disabled people get the equipment they needed. I expanded my operation and now have two trucks to deliver, and pick up equipment.'

Shirley admired this man because he took his own life as an example, so he could help other disadvantaged people. The only thing she disliked about Darren was that he smoked.

When they were in her car one time, he asked her whether he might smoke in her car. She tapped a little sign she'd put on the dash of her car that said, 'No smoking.'

'I'm allergic to cigarette smoke,' she admitted, and I don't want smoke in my home or my car because I don't want to expose my children to the fumes.'

He put away his cigarette case and didn't ask her again whether he could smoke near her. She didn't know till several months later that he'd quit smoking that very day, and never lit up another cigarette in his lifetime.

They dated casually for a while until her life changed when Ernie Larson phoned her at home. 'Well, I've done it. I've moved out on my wife and am living with a buddy on a little acreage on the outskirts of Edmonton. I've also started the proceedings towards getting divorced,' he explained, 'Will you go out with me now?'

She laughed and replied, 'It sounds like you've made some major changes in your life. Yes, I'd like to go out with you.'

They dated for a month and enjoyed each other's company. One day he asked whether he could see her the next night and she had to turn him down by saying, 'I have to go to Edson and stay overnight. They're having problems in one of the nearby relay stations, so I won't be in Edmonton.'

'That's ironic. I have a client there that I've been putting off seeing. Shall I see if he'll see me tomorrow and we can have dinner together?'

'Sounds like a good plan. My co-worker and I will be staying at the Edson Inn – separate rooms of course, and I'd love to have dinner with you. When we check in, I'll find out what room you'll be in and will call you to let you know we're back from the relay station. I doubt if we'll be late, but it's possible we might be.'

'Okay, I'll wait for you to call me at the Inn,' he promised.

That evening, Shirley looked over her wardrobe trying to decide what she would wear when she saw Ernie the next day. She knew that her work clothes would not be suitable, and finally decided to wear her new turquoise silk slacks and matching top. 'This outfit is casual, but dressy,' she thought as she realized that she was looking forward to having dinner with him. She carefully packed it in her suitcase.

As Shirley described in her book, she was blown away by the attraction they felt towards each other and both were flabbergasted when they found themselves in her bed at the Inn. They made mad passionate love most of the night and both were sated and tired by the morning. Arrangements had been made for her to have breakfast with her co-worker, and she asked whether someone could join them. The two men shook hands, and her co-worker could tell that they were more than just friends.

'We bumped into each other in the restaurant last night,' Shirley lied. Her co-worker had decided to have room service that night, so she'd been free to join Ernie for dinner.

Their romance had bloomed, and Ernie obtained his divorce. By this time, they were spending as much time with each other as possible. Because she still had her daughter at home, they spent most of their lovemaking time at his home in the country. Shirley suddenly realized that for the first time in her life she was in love. The relationship she'd had with her battering husband had not been love – this was love.

One evening after they'd had dinner, Ernie looked upset and Shirley asked him, 'What's the matter? You look upset?'

His reply devastated her. 'I've just realized that I've jumped out of one relationship with my wife directly into another with you and wonder if it was a good move on my part.'

Shirley's heart was thumping when she asked, 'What do you want to do?'

'I think we should back off from each other for a while, so I can get my head on straight again,' he admitted sheepishly.

Although that was not what she wanted to do, she agreed that they would not see each other for a while. She waited four months, then learned that he was engaged to a secretary in his office and wondered if their relationship had been going on when he was seeing her. After learning of his relationship, she didn't date anyone for over six months as she tried to heal her hurt feelings.

A co-worker of hers noticed that Shirley wasn't going out socially any more and asked her if she would like to meet someone her husband worked with. The man was several years older than Shirley but was a judge in the courts. Her co-worker had shown him Shirley's picture and he said he'd like to meet her. So, it was arranged.

They met at the Westin Hotel and had a lovely dinner. Shirley didn't feel any real attraction to him, but he was an intelligent man and an interesting conversationalist. When he learned that it was her birthday the next day, he asked whether he could take her out for dinner again. She agreed to do so. He also mentioned that he was on the lookout for a new investment property, and knowing where she lived, asked whether there were any apartments for sale in her building.

'As it happens, the unit next door to mine is for sale and because it's a mirror to the one I live in, you could get an idea of what it looks like if you saw mine' she suggested.

He agreed to come to her apartment before they went out to dinner. When he rang the security buzzer of her building, she let him in and gave him a tour of her apartment. He admired the unit and asked her for a person he could contact about the unit for sale. It was vacant now because the woman was in palliative care as she battled cancer.

They had a lovely dinner and he asked her if he could see the view from her apartment when it was dark. She lived on the sixteenth floor in a unit that had thirty-two feet of picture windows that overlooked the river valley. The view was spectacular, especially at night. When they reached her apartment, he gallantly took her keys and opened the door. He did gasp at the sight. Before they'd left for dinner it had still been daylight, so this was another spectacular scene. They enjoyed a cup of tea and then he gave her a peck on her cheek and left her apartment.

The next morning, Shirley's phone rang. It was him. He said, 'Do you always give men your keys?'

Shirley was taken aback and went to her purse to get her keys. They weren't there – he had them!

'I was tempted to come over during the night and let myself into your apartment to show you how dangerous it is to give a stranger the keys to your home.'

Shirley realized that she had to get them back. She was furious at his comments and wondered what had ever possessed him to put the keys in his pocket instead of giving them back to her. She also realized that she had to remain calm and find a solution to the problem.

'I need my keys. I must take my daughter shopping for some things she needs for school. Can you drop them over to me?'

He agreed to do so and said he would be there within the hour. When he rang her unit, but instead of letting him through the security door, she went down in the elevator and met him. He handed her the keys, then she erupted, 'Do you have any idea what you've done? And do you realize that if you had broken into my apartment last night you wouldn't have come out alive. I have karate, Judo and Tae Kwan Do,' she said as she slammed the entrance door in his face.

As soon as she returned to her apartment, she called the building maintenance people of the building and asked whether she could have the locks on her door changed. They sent a locksmith and billed her one hundred and fifty dollars, but she felt safer knowing that if he had copied her keys, he couldn't get into her unit. She knew that he would not be able to copy the security door lock because it was a special key. She just hoped that he didn't buy the unit across the hall from her and warned the management of the building about her episode with him. She also told her co-worker what she thought about the 'date' she'd arranged with the man.

'I guess you can't even trust judges these days,' she thought as she again went into hibernation date-wise.

Shirley's book went on to discuss situations that happened to her as she raised her children as a single parent. Some were very funny – others rather sad as her children moved away to begin their lives as working adults.

Becky put the book down. She knew that Jim was anxious to know how good it was, so after she finished editing it, she phoned him.'

'Hi Jim; it's Becky. I've finished editing Shirley's second book 'Love, Life, Living,' she announced. She had completed it much sooner than he thought it would be finished.

'What do you think of it?' was his cautious question.

'It's as good as the first one. She expects to do more work on it, but basically, it's a good book. At the end it leaves some things wide open for another sequel to be written, so we're in for a batch of good books from this writer.'

'Glad to hear it. By the way, the tour is going great guns. The sales are beginning to come in as Shirley goes across Canada. We can hardly keep up with the demand, so we're doing another print run of the book. I hope the same thing happens when she goes to the States – that's where the biggest sales will be. Let's cross our fingers that she keeps up her energy to keep doing such good interviews. I saw a couple of them, and she's great on camera – much better than last time.'

'Good for her. She did tell me she felt much more confident this time, so she's obviously feeling much more at home in front of a camera or microphone.'

'I'll keep you informed of her progress. In the meantime, I have another book for you to edit. Do you feel up to doing another one?'

'Sure – send it over. Shirley's approval of my edits for 'Love, Life, Living,' won't be done for at least a month, so I have time to do another book in the meantime.'

Chapter 19

As usual, Dan delivered Mike to spend the weekend with Emily and her parents. Emily asked him to stay for a few minutes, then said, 'I've improved so much that I've decided to move into my own apartment. I'll have a carer stay with me for a while but I'm getting around quite well now.'

'I'm glad to hear that,' he responded, 'but are you sure you're ready to take that step?'

'Yes, I feel terrible making my parents look after me. The money I earn selling my paintings, plus doing the accounts for a small firm, will give me a steady income, so I feel I can manage financially on my own.'

'It sounds as if you'll do well with those two incomes. What do your parents think about this?' he asked.

'They're all for it, but say they'll miss me and having Mike come every second weekend as we've done in the past,' she said. 'I've decided that we're at the point where I want you to consider giving me joint custody of Mike,' she said watching his reaction, then continued, 'The way I think it will work best, would be for me to have Mike one week and you have him the next, and so on.'

'He's going to be going to kindergarten fairly soon. How will you manage that?' he asked.

'I can have my carer drop him off and pick him up and I don't think it will be long until I can drive him myself. My balance is much better, and I have good strength in my legs, but still have a way to go before I can trust myself to be able to react quickly enough to get my foot from the gas to the brake if needed. My rehab trainer is working on that,' she added proudly.

Dan hoped she was right. He'd hate to see her have another accident, and of course he was concerned about the welfare of his son Mike who might be in the car with her. 'I guess we'll have to change the custody agreement. Are you sure you're ready for that responsibility?' he asked seriously.

'I won't want things to change until I've been on my own for about a month. I want to see how things go. I also want to make sure that I've hired the right carer; someone who will be the right person to look after Mike properly.'

'Well, let me know when you want to do this, and we can change the custody agreement,' he agreed.

It took Emily a month to find a suitable apartment that didn't have stairs and had easy access but was close to Mike's kindergarten. Then it took another month to find and test out the carer she hired to assist her and transport Mike to and from kindergarten.

Finally, things fell into place and she phoned Dan to let him know that things were ready. They planned to see Dan's lawyer to change the custody agreement. At this point, there was no need for them both to have lawyers; they just needed one to change the court custody agreement. The next week Dan delivered Mike to Emily's new apartment. Dan had explained the arrangement they'd made, and Mike was quite pleased with it although he did say, 'Will I still be seeing Grandpa and Grandma?'

'Of course you will. When you see your Mom, you'll likely visit them, or they'll visit you.'

That seemed to appease Mike because he did love his grandparents. Emily and Dan both went to Mike's kindergarten and explained to the manager about their arrangement and gave them a calendar explaining when each parent would have custody of Mike. Emily also produced a picture of her carer and explained that she would be delivering and picking him up while he stayed with her; at least for the present until she was able to safely obtain a driver's licence herself.

Sandy and Becky missed Mike when he was with Emily, but having baby Vicki on the scene, they soon adjusted to his weekly absences.

Three months later, Emily's rehabilitation trainer said he thought she was ready to get her driver's licence back. He wrote a letter stating her improved abilities, and after she'd passed the driving part of the test, she was given her driver's licence. She and her parents celebrated that night knowing she was on her way to being 'normal' again.

The next day she felt so good that she sat down to make other goals she'd like to reach. Now that she didn't need a carer, she decided that she would still like someone's help with any heavy tasks that needed doing around her apartment, so she hired a housekeeper to come in once a week to assist with those chores.

Another goal she made was to become a better artist and knew that the best way to make this happen was to take advanced painting classes. She'd learned about a local artist, Albert Guida, who was making a name for himself and when she saw two of his paintings at the art gallery, she decided to take the chance of contacting him.

After working up her courage, she phoned him. 'Hello Mr Guida, my name is Emily Jeffries. I'm wondering if you work with budding artists? I've had some success, but know I can do better,' she said in a rush.

'I haven't done teaching, but could consider it,' he said with his foreign accent. Emily thought it sounded French but didn't sound like the Quebecois French she was used to hearing on Canadian television.

'I'd need to see what you've done so far, to see whether I could be of help to you,' he added.

'When can we meet? I could bring some of my paintings over. I've sold several of them but took photographs of them before I did. I could bring those as well,' she suggested.

'That would be fine. I have a small studio where we can meet.' He gave her the address which was in the area where she often bought items in the little boutique shops in a Yuppie area of Edmonton.

He then suggested, 'Would tomorrow at ten be suitable for you?'

'Yes, it would, she replied than asked, 'Do you have anyone at your end that could carry the boxes of paintings into your studio? I'm not able to lift heavy things but have someone at my end that can put them into my car before I leave.'

'I'm quite fit myself and I'd be glad to do that for you.' He wondered if she was disabled in some way but was too much of a gentleman to ask.

When Emily arrived the next morning, she entered the studio and was greeted by an extremely good-looking man that she judged to be in his late forties. He as well gave a second look at this lovely lady who said she was an artist. This would be an interesting meeting.

'Hello, I'm Emily Jeffries,' she said as she extended her hand. 'And you must be Albert.'

They shook hands; he smiled and said, 'Nice to meet you. Let's get those paintings. I'm anxious to see them'

She led him out to her car and pointed to the two boxes of paintings. He made two trips getting them into his studio. On the second trip, she picked up her photo portfolio of paintings she'd already sold. Albert carefully took the paintings out of their boxes and placed them around the room. She could see from the smile on his face that he liked them, but he also frowned when he examined one of them. Without commenting on the paintings, he asked to see the portfolio of photos. He examined them carefully and spent considerable time looking at the photos of the charcoal sketches of Mike.

'These are excellent. You say you sold them? What a pity. I hope you got what they were worth?' he emphasized.

'I didn't sell these ones. They're sketches of my son Mike when he was younger. His father and his wife have the actual drawings displayed on their walls at their home.'

'Ah,' he said. 'Do you have a photograph of your son, so I can compare them to the sketches?'

Emily pulled out her wallet and extracted a small picture of Mike as he looked now.

He examined his picture then smiled and said, 'You have talent in this area. You should do more charcoal sketches.'

'That's about the only ones I've done of people. Most of the other charcoal sketches I've done are of inanimate things, but I did feel good about the ones I did of Mike,' she added with a blush.

'You should be proud of them. I think you could make a lot of money doing portraits. Have you ever done cartoons that depict people where others know the picture is of them, but they're in funny situations?' he asked.

'I don't know what you mean?' she replied.

'Well, for instance, doing a sketch of a person, but giving them a little body sitting on a toboggan or skateboard – something funny that people can enjoy laughing at.'

'I guess I could try that. Maybe I can do more of Mike and possibly his teen-aged stepsister Sandy, and if they go well, I can ask Mike's dad and step-mom if they'll let me do one of them.'

'Why don't you do that and when you get them done, I'd like you to show them to me. Now I'd like to comment on each of your paintings.'

He walked around the room and after he examined each painting, he gave suggestions on how the paintings could be improved. When he got to the one where he had frowned earlier, he said, 'There's something tragic about this painting. It seems to be a collage of several scenes. Can you explain it to me?'

'Well, this is showing my car upside down in the bushes. I was in a terrible car accident and woke up paralysed from the waist down. The second scene is me sitting in a wheel chair, although I've disguised my face. The third scene is me on the parallel bars trying to walk – where I again disguised my face. So, the entire picture shows the accident and the aftermath. I thought it was a cheerful one, but I see that the dark colours I used in the painting show how depressed I was at the time I painted it. It's one that has not sold even though I painted it quite some time ago,' she explained keeping eye contact with him to see his reaction.

'It looks as if you've had quite a life so far. I'm glad to see that your progress has continued. If I were you, I would not display that painting. It actually shows anguish and pain, and most people would not want to have that kind of emotion in a painting they purchased,' he said watching her reaction.

'You're right. I hesitated to bring that one along but thought I should do so to get your reaction. Thanks for being so honest about my paintings. I'll put this one in the back of the cupboard, or maybe I'll just throw it out because I'm not in that space any more.'

'You do that. Purge your soul of that experience and concentrate on the fact that you have recovered – and recovered remarkably well,' he added enjoying the look of her. 'Paint about that joyous situation,' he suggested.

'I will. But first I think I'll have some fun doing the charcoal sketches. That sounds like it could be something that will cheer everyone up including me!' she exclaimed laughingly.

'How much do I owe you for your time?' she asked as he began placing the paintings back in their boxes.

'Nothing but I hope you will keep showing me what you're doing.'

Albert carefully carried the boxes out to her car.

'Thank you again Albert. I really appreciate your help.'

'That's Al; Albert sounds so stuffy. I like my friends to call me Al, and I hope we can remain friends. I'm looking forward to seeing your future works of art' he said with a smile.

They shook hands again and Emily drove home with a smile on her face. She was going to have fun doing the cartoon sketches and couldn't wait till she could start sketching Mike when he came next week.

She found doing the cartoons so much fun, that she did one every day depicting the goofy things that Mike did. She still did a full portrait of his face but gave him a little body doing unusual things. Her first one was of him eating spaghetti where he had spaghetti sauce all over his face and shirt. She gave him a big grin and they both laughed when she finished it.

Every day she found something funny to draw and every evening she showed the sketch to Mike. He loved them, and so did she. By Friday evening she had five of them and decided to phone Al about them. 'Can I bring them around to show you on Monday?' she asked.

'Of course you can. Why don't you come to my studio after you drop Mike off at Kindergarten that morning? I'll have coffee ready for you.'

'I'll see you then,' she promised.

She had him turn his back while she displayed her sketches. When he turned around, he started to laugh and by the time he saw the last one, he turned to Emily and gave her a big hug. 'They're exactly what I wanted you to do. See how much fun they are? I wish I had your talent for doing this. You're on your way. You'll have hundreds of people wanting this kind of sketch for their walls. Well done!' he ended.

She blushed, mainly because of the hug, because she realized that she responded sexually to that hug and would like more of them. 'Thanks for the praise. I was so busy last week showing you my paintings that I didn't take time to see any of yours. Do you have any here that I can see?'

'As it happens, I too have been busy lately and have just finished doing a portrait of the premier of our province.' He brought it out and placed it on an easel. 'What do you think?' he asked rather shyly.

Emily gazed in wonder at the painting. The painting was an exact duplicate of their premier. She gasped as she acknowledged the wonder of his ability, 'It's him. It's him! You've captured him exactly. When did he sit for this portrait?' she asked.

'He didn't. I've done it from watching him on television and just had a short interview with him when he asked whether I could do the portrait. That was just two weeks ago Friday and I got busy right away – and here it is. He has no idea that it's ready, but I wanted you to see it before I showed it to him,' he admitted shyly.

'He'll be absolutely amazed as will everyone else. I hope you'll be given a good commission for doing it – it's truly a work of art!' she gushed.

It was his turn to blush. 'Thanks. I needed that. As you know, an artist always questions his or her talents, and I'm pleased that you like it. Before I show him, I'll choose a proper frame and then I'll phone his office to see when he wants to see it.'

'I'd love to know what he thinks of it. Will you phone me and let me know his reaction?' she queried.

'Yes, I will. I have your number and will phone you after I show it to him. In the meantime, do you have any other victims in mind for doing the cartoon sketches?'

'I'll show my ex-husband Dan these sketches and ask him whether I could do some of him, his wife Becky and their daughter Sandy. They also have a baby, but I don't think it would be appropriate for me to do that kind of sketch of her. I might, however, do a full portrait of her as she is,' she said, thinking out loud.

'Okay, we both have things to do. Let's keep in touch,' he said as he gave her a peck on her cheek. Again, she felt that tug of pleasure, and turned his face to give his other cheek a kiss.

'That's how they do it in France isn't it?' she teased. She'd gone on Google and learned that he was divorced, had lived in Paris for many years and had immigrated to Canada ten years ago.

His eyes lit up, 'Yes, it is. Both cheeks and when one is cheeky, we even do this,' he said as he gave her a soft gentle kiss on the lips.

'I hope you don't mind me doing that, but you are a very attractive lady, and we seem to have so much in common' he admitted.

'Yes, we do, and no, I didn't mind at all.'

'Would you like to have dinner one night this week?' he asked.

'I'd really enjoy that.'

And so, began the romance of Emily and Albert. Before she put a new painting up for sale, she had Albert examine it and often made minor changes to the painting. One time after making suggestions, Albert said, 'I'll be going to France in two weeks for an Art exhibition. Would you consider coming with me?'

Emily was surprised that he would ask her but knew that it was not within her budget to go with him. She shook her head and said sadly, 'I'd love to have gone with you, but I'm afraid I can't.'

'Is it your week to have your son?' he asked.

'No, that week he will be with his dad.'

'Then, why can't you come?' he pleaded.

She looked down as she said, 'I simply can't afford such a luxury even though it would be a wonderful experience to be there.'

'Would you consider letting me buy your ticket and paying for your room at the hotel?' he asked.

'Oh, I couldn't let you do that,' she replied shaking her head.

'Why not? I've grown fond of you and would like to give that gift to you knowing how much it would mean to you. Are you sure you won't re-consider?'

Emily mulled it over, then thought, 'This is a once in a lifetime opportunity. I should take it, and I like Al and know he'll be a gentleman during our trip.'

She looked up at him and nodded yes.

'You've made me very happy,' he admitted. 'Let me make arrangements.'

A few minutes later, after talking to his travel agent, it was all arranged. Al had to change the seat he had chosen so they could sit beside each other on the plane. Emily was surprised to learn that they would be flying business class. It would be the longest trip Emily had ever been on. Their flight left Edmonton at eleven thirty-five in the morning, so they had to be at the airport by eight that morning which added another three hours to their travel time. They would stop over in Montreal and change planes and would arrive in Paris the same day at five thirty-five. However, in their heads, it would be one thirty-five – just after midnight when they would arrive. They'd both been able to sleep on the plane and hoped to get into the Paris time zone as soon as possible, so decided to stay up till Paris bedtime.

When they arrived at the Hyatt Paris Madelene Hotel, they first went to their rooms to unpack their suitcases and then met at the hotel restaurant. Al had stopped off at a little shop in the hotel and had purchased a red long-stemmed rose that he gave her when he met her at the restaurant. She was thrilled at the romantic gesture. He'd also picked up several brochures about tours they could take in Paris.

Al handed the brochures to Emily and suggested that they book themselves in to see three of them. The Art show was just one day, so they had several days to enjoy Paris. Emily read over the brochures and smiled as she read them. The first was a trip to Loire Valley Castle. The brochure stated:

The day dedicated to "Renaissance" starts with a visit of Amboise Castle, where King Francis 1st welcomed Leonardo Da Vinci at the end of his life. After lunch (included), you leave for Chenonceau Castle and the day finishes with a visit of Chambord. The trip highlights:

- Small group Loire Valley tour from Paris by minivan
- Enjoy lunch after a visit of Amboise Castle
- Discover Chenonceau Castle that is built on the River Cher
- Visit the Chateau of Chambord (Chambord Castle) and enjoy panoramic views from the grounds
- Small group tour for a more personalized experience
- Hotel pick-up and drop-off by minivan

'That one sounds very nice,' she commented as she handed that brochure back to Al. Then she read the next one that talked about the Moulin Rouge Show:

The Moulin Rouge is the number one show in Paris, if not the whole of Europe. No wonder it sells out quickly! Don't miss your chance to see the world-renowned showgirls and French

Cancan dancers strut their stuff on the Moulin Rouge's historic stage. Highlights of the show:

- Moulin Rouge Paris cabaret theatre show
- Cancan dancers and fabulous costumes, music and settings
- Choice of two show times with champagne
- Choice of dinner and show or show and champagne
- Moulin Rouge Paris at night is a must-see!

Moulin Rouge Paris is selling out fast! Lido and_ Paradis Latin cabaret shows in Paris still available. Book Now!

She nodded her head and handed that one back to him, then examined the third one that was about a Paris one day sightseeing tour:

To experience the best of Paris in a single day, take this Paris "walking tour" tour with a difference! You'll travel by river shuttle and visit Paris' most famous riverside monuments on this comprehensive full-day tour, including guided visits to the Louvre Museum, Notre Dame Cathedral and lunch at the Eiffel Tower. Highlights are:

- See the best of Paris on a one-day tour
- Guided visits to the Louvre Museum and Notre Dame Cathedral
- Lunch at the 58 Tour Eiffel restaurant at the Eiffel Tower
- Two Seine River cruises to the Eiffel Tower and Notre Dame Cathedral

'These all sound like great trips. Which one do you want to go on?' she queried.

'All of them! I want you to really see what Paris is all about and I want to treat you to them!'

'You're far too generous,' she said blushing.

He took her hand and said, 'You're an important part of my life now and I want to make you happy.'

They enjoyed their meal, and it was after eleven when they said goodnight. To ensure that they had a good night's sleep, they'd both taken melatonin tablets that had been recommended by Al's doctor which would help them fight jet lag. They'd taken one pill an hour before they left the restaurant, then took another just before they slipped into their respective beds.

Emily was smiling as she snuggled down into the luxury of her hotel bed. Everything was so romantic, and she couldn't wait to sightsee and view all the lovely paintings at the Art show.

They spent a wonderful week in Paris and Emily loved seeing all the paintings. The evening after they'd been at the Moulin Rouge Show, they paused outside her door and it seemed natural for her to invite him in to spend the night with her. The next day, they cancelled his room, and he moved his things into hers.

Their flight back to Edmonton was going to leave at eight fifty-five in the evening, so they had to be at the airport three hours before it left. That afternoon they decided to have a late lunch before they left their hotel.

Al reached across the table and took Emily's hand. 'I've thoroughly enjoyed our holiday. I've been so glad you could come with me on this trip.'

'I've loved every minute of it myself. I keep pinching myself to remind myself that I'm in the magical city of Paris. It lives up to its reputation and I'm so glad you brought me here.'

'The pleasure is all mine. It's a rather romantic place – wouldn't you agree?'

She looked down knowing that he'd swept her off her feet with his romantic ways. 'Yes, I've seen a side of you I didn't know existed. You're a very romantic man.'

'Well, I did live in Paris for several years and it's a catchy disease,' he said as he smiled tenderly at her. He reached into his pocket and removed a small box. Emily's eyes spotted it and she knew what was going to happen next. When he said, 'Will you marry me?' she wasn't surprised.

'This is awfully sudden!' she said putting her hand to her throat, 'I don't know what to say.'

'I hope you'll say yes. Why don't you think about it as we fly home and hopefully you can give me an answer by the time we get back to Edmonton. I'll ask you again just before we land. Would that be okay with you?' he asked, watching her face.

'Yes, I'll give you my answer then,' she promised as he put the ring back in his pocket.

It was hard for them both to sleep on the way home. Again, they changed planes in Montreal, and it was just about to land in Edmonton at nine thirty-five in the morning when Al turned to her and she simply nodded her head. He gave her a big hug and asked whether he could put the ring on her finger. She nodded again. He soon saw that it was far too big for her finger and promised to have it sized right away.

They were both smiling when Emily's parents picked them up at the airport. Little Mike was with them, and he rushed into his mother's arms. 'I missed you Mommy!' he babbled.

'I missed you too baby,' she crooned.

'Not a baby!' he said with his hands on his hips.

Emily turned to Al with a questioning look as she sat beside Mike in his car seat. She pointed at her ring finger and he nodded. She tapped her mother's shoulder and she turned around where she was sitting in the passenger seat.

'We have something to tell you.' Emily started. 'We've become engaged,' she said patting Al's hand.

Her mother was pleased. She liked Al and thought he was a good influence on her daughter, and they seemed to have lots in common.

'Congratulations,' she and Emily's father said simultaneously.

Her mother added, 'Have you set a date for your wedding?'

'Not yet Mom. I just agreed to marry him half an hour ago!' she revealed.

'Well let us know. We'd like to set it up for you if you'd let us.'

'I'd be pleased to pay for the wedding,' revealed Al. Her parents had paid for her first wedding to Dan, and it didn't seem right to Al that they pay for another wedding.

Then he added, 'I personally don't want a big one because most of my family are scattered around the globe.'

When Emily and Al met the next day, to discuss when they would like to get married, they decided they'd like a Christmas wedding. He would pay for the wedding, but Emily's mother would finalize the plans for the wedding. Emily debated whether she would invite Dan and his family to the wedding and decided that they had such a good relationship with each other that they should be invited.

The wedding went without a hitch and they were pronounced man and wife two days after Christmas. They decided to wait until summer to take their real honeymoon but spent the next week in Florida where it was lovely and warm. That summer they returned to Paris and that's where Emily found out that she was pregnant. So, another baby was added to the mix and Mike was very excited when he learned that he would soon have a little brother.

Chapter 20

Shirley's book tour was over, and everyone at Becky's publishing firm was elated at the amount of sales she'd generated. They were pleased to tell her that her book was now listed as a best-seller. One of their representatives had been to an international book fair in Europe and had highlighted Shirley's book. She'd successfully interested several international book publishers to translate and release her book in their languages.

Jim was able to tell Shirley that they expected to receive agreements from United States and United Kingdom publishers who would release the book in English. The UK publisher distributed their books to over sixty countries, so that was a coup for Shirley. Next came a request to publish in Russian, then hot on the heels of that offer came ones from Lithuania, Romania, Serbia, Poland, Spain, Japan, and China publishing companies. Shirley was on a roll and Jim was kept busy negotiating for royalty percentages and trying to convince the publishing companies to offer the books in eBook format as well.

Soon the royalties were pouring in and Shirley decided to take a sabbatical from her job. Jim convinced her that it would be a good idea to wait for six months to release her second book 'Love, Life, Living,' when he would plan another book tour. Again, Becky did the planning, but did not actually go on the tour with Shirley – it was far too extensive a tour for her to leave her baby and family.

When Shirley got back from her tour, she got busy writing the third sequel to her book which was all about when she started her own business entitled 'Upwards and Onwards.' Becky couldn't wait to receive it.

In the interim, Becky worked on finishing her own book. One Thursday night at dinner she looked at her handsome husband and said, 'I finished it!'

He looked at her wondering what she meant. 'Finished what?' he enquired.

'I finished my book. I finished it yesterday and proof read it today. I think it's now ready for Jim to have one of his other editors go through it and evaluate it,' she added.

'You promised I could read it first,' he reminded her.

'I know I promised that to you. That's why I'm mentioning it to you tonight. When do you think you'll have time to read it?' she enquired.

'How about doing it this weekend? I'm not on call at the station, so hopefully I can read it and you can send it to Jim on Monday. How does that sound?'

'Great. I want you to be brutally honest and tell me truthfully what you think of my book. Don't mince words – tell it like it is. Will you promise to do that?'

'Okay, I promise.'

Becky left the room and returned with the printed manuscript. 'I thought you might want to read it this way, so you don't have to do it on the computer. Feel free to make any notations in the margins. I'll be sending it to Jim in file format so the person who's editing it can make changes throughout the manuscript.'

Becky was on edge that weekend knowing that Dan was holed up in their office examining her manuscript. When he surfaced for lunch, she waited anxiously for him to make comments, but he talked about everything except about the book and she began to wonder if he was not pleased with its contents. The book told him a lot about her background before she met him, about her teenage exploits and her shenanigans as a rowdy teenager. She'd even mentioned that she'd tried marijuana when she was a stupid sixteen-year-old and wondered how he would react to that piece of information. It wasn't until after dinner and he'd spent another two hours devouring the book that he spoke to her.

'Well?' was all she said as he entered the living room with the manuscript in his hands. He knew what she wanted to know.

'I certainly learned a lot about you and your life before you met me,' he admitted, not committing himself to giving her the information he knew she wanted.

'Did you make any notations through the manuscript?' she enquired, trying to get him to talk about it honestly.

'Yes, I did in a couple of places,' he admitted.

'Don't keep me in suspense,' she begged as she wrung her hands.

'I'll put you out of your misery. It's more of a book that women would read than men, but it's well written and I was kept interested in it until the very end. I think you have a winner!' he finally admitted giving her a big hug.

'Oh, I'm so glad. I was afraid you might not like it or hate me because of some of the stuff I've spoken about in the book,' she added.

'Did you really try marijuana?' he asked incredulously. He knew what an advocate Becky was now that children and adults stay clear of any kind of mind-altering drug.

'Once was enough. I didn't like feeling out of control, and the time I took it, I felt out of control. My thoughts were muddled, and I felt as if I was someone else. I didn't like it at all and vowed I'd never try another drug in my lifetime.'

'Glad to hear you learned that lesson and I'm glad it wasn't one of these new synthetic drugs you decided to try.'

'Thank goodness they weren't available then and most kids would only try marijuana and most of the kids I associated with stayed away from the hard stuff.'

When she arrived at work on Monday, she asked Jim if she could speak with him about a new author. She handed the USB drive that held her manuscript and placed it in his hands. He looked up rather surprised that she was the one giving him the manuscript when it was normally him giving her one to edit for another author.

'Where did you get this?' he asked, if maybe the receptionist had asked her to deliver it to him.

'It's a book I wrote,' she admitted, 'and wonder if you would have one of the other editors look at it and evaluate it,' she concluded sheepishly. She didn't know what Jim would think about her – one of his editors – being the one to write a book.

'Would you like me to look at it first?' he asked.

'I'd appreciate that. Dan read it this weekend and he liked it but did admit it was more a book that women would buy. I really would like your expert opinion on how good or bad it really is.'

He promised to read the book as soon as he had time. 'In the meantime, here's a new book for you to edit,' he said as he handed her another USB drive. 'Another new author we've decided to look at.'

Becky returned home and began editing the book but kept being side-tracked wondering what Jim thought about her book. It didn't take her long to edit the book and decided that it was not one that her company should publish. The author seemed to deviate from the plot too often which left the reader lost at times wondering what he was talking about. She decided to phone Jim about her findings.

'Hi Jim; it's Becky. I've read over the manuscript and wanted to give you my opinion of it.' she said.

'You did that one in a hurry,' he said.

'Yes, unfortunately, it isn't a book I'd recommend we publish. I got lost many times throughout the book wondering what the author was talking about. He jumped from topic to topic and I found myself getting frustrated wondering what happened to characters mentioned earlier in the book. So, no, I don't recommend this book.'

'Thanks for your evaluation of it. Now I have the awful task of letting a budding writer know that we can't accept his book. I'll need a synopsis from you about what was wrong with the book, and hopefully he will understand what he has to do to repair it or write another one that's better,' he ended.

Becky took a big breath and broached the subject that was foremost in her mind. 'Have you been able to start reading my book?'

'As a matter of fact, I'm sitting here reading it right now, but I've just started reading it, so can't make an evaluation at this point,' he said as her heart fell.

Jim didn't want to give an evaluation until he'd finished reading it but knew how anxious Becky must feel about what he thought about her work. 'If I don't have too many interruptions, I should be able to finish it by tomorrow or the next day,' he promised.

When the phone rang, Becky somehow knew it was Jim and when she looked at the caller display her guess had been correct. 'Hi Jim,' she said.

'Hi yourself. Well, I've finished the book and I like it. There are some things I think can be improved and have noted them as I went through the manuscript. I'm going to e-mail you with the changes that I've highlighted in red font. I think one of your chapters should be moved to another area, but otherwise it is a good first book.'

Becky realized that he had not raved about the book, so knew that it was a 'so-so' book with a bit of potential, so knew she would have to re-think some sections of the book and pay attention to the suggestions Jim had made through the manuscript. She now knew what it felt like to have her work assessed and realized that like most authors she almost felt that her book was part of her and if it was rejected – she was rejected. She vowed to remember that when she evaluated books in the future.

When she received Jim's e-mail with the edited book enclosure, she did a re-write of some sections of the book. When that was completed, she sent it back to Jim and was pleased that he thought it was greatly improved. After Becky signed an agreement for them to publish her book and realized the level of elation an author could feel when his or her first book was published.

That evening she and Dan opened a bottle of red wine and celebrated the event. Soon it would be her turn to go on a book tour. Because she was now the author, another woman at her firm set up the interviews for her and Becky was kept busy planning to be away from home for the two weeks it took to go across Canada doing interviews.

Her book was moderately successful but did not take off like an author would wish and she decided to concentrate her future efforts on helping other authors get their books published, rather than spend her time writing books herself. She was glad of the experience but decided she wouldn't do it again.

Chapter 21

Becky's phone rang, and it was Jim again and she wondered whether he had another book for her to edit.

'Hi Becky; I've got good news! We've been negotiating with several movie film makers and have just signed an agreement to have Shirley's first book made into a movie. She's over the moon about it but was a bit disappointed when I told her she would have to work with a screen writer. She thought they would just take the comments shown in the book and make it exactly like she wrote it. Could you explain to her how this works? She'll likely call you quite soon. In the meantime, the movie studio is talking with screen writers and hopefully they'll find one who can work with Shirley to get her story told. I've recommended that the screen writer be a woman, so Shirley's story can be seen from the point of view of a battered woman. They've agreed to use the title of the book 'Broken Dreams' for the movie title as well,' he concluded.

'Okay, I'll talk with her. If she doesn't call me today, I'll call her tomorrow to explain why we need to involve a screen writer. I think once she accepts that it's necessary, she'll cooperate. Like most authors, she wants to make sure that the book contents are depicted correctly and not sensationalized by the screen writer. I'll let you know what happens when I talk to her,' she promised.

'Thanks for that.'

'Did you get her a good contract money-wise?' Becky asked.

'Yes, she will be sitting pretty after it comes out.

'Will we have any say in how the movie is depicted?'

'We'll have final say on the film script. I'm sure it'll be a good movie and will highlight what a terrible epidemic we have world-wide with domestic violence and child abuse. It will be aimed, of course, towards an adult audience and will be rather graphic when it shows the beatings she withstood during the marriage. This movie will show actual wife battering. It will differ from the psychological kind of wife abuse that was shown in the movie 'Sleeping with the enemy' that starred Julia Roberts that came out in 1991,' he added.

Later that afternoon Shirley phoned, and they discussed in length why it was necessary for them to have a screen writer. When Shirley eventually met with the screen writer, she was fascinated to see the story boards that were put together for the cast of the movie to follow. It showed how each little scene in the movie would be shot; showed the camera angle, the lighting, where the stars would sit, stand, or lie and in general told everyone on the set what was expected of them.

The film makers decided to film the movie in Edmonton, so it would be more authentic. Because some of the scenes took place in the dead of winter when it was very cold, Edmonton was an ideal place to film it. When they started filming the movie, Shirley asked Becky if she would like to watch them do a few scenes. Before Shirley called her, she obtained permission from the producer to have Becky watch a few scenes by explaining, 'She's the one who edited my book and it became a best-seller, so I'd like her to be able to watch some of the scenes in the movie.' They granted permission.

Becky was quite excited that she would be able to see an actual movie being filmed. Because she'd played an integral part in getting it accepted, she wondered what she would find when they got to where the scene was being filmed. She was thankful that it was an indoor shot.

The scene she watched was being filmed in a studio that duplicated a room in the home where Shirley had lived. There were a lot of people involved, and Becky was mesmerized as she watched the scene progress. She recognized that this scene was where Shirley had first been hit by her husband. The actors did the scene over and over, and finally were given a break before they tried it again. Time after time, something went awry, and the producer wanted the scene to be perfect.

At the break, Becky was introduced to the two main characters that were playing the parts of Shirley and her husband. Becky was amazed how close the woman resembled Shirley. Becky had never met Shirley's husband, so she asked Shirley whether he resembled her husband.

'He's really close in looks,' Shirley agreed.

Becky shook the actors' hands when she was introduced, and blushed when Shirley said, 'If it wasn't for this lady, this movie would not have been made. She's the person who edited my book and recommended it to her publishing company.'

'Good for you,' boomed the man representing Shirley's husband. 'Without you, we wouldn't have this job – thanks.' They all enjoyed a cup of coffee and Danish.

Soon it was time for them to get back to work on filming 'Broken Dreams' and this time the scene was done perfectly. Then it was time to get ready for the next scene. Becky could see how technical and time-consuming it was to film a movie. Each scene took at least ten times and sometimes twenty times as long as it appeared in the movie. She marvelled at the expertise of the make-up artists who were able to show the bruises and abrasions that Shirley supposedly suffered after her husband had hit her for the first time. It certainly looked real, and the actors really had her feeling that the woman had been severely battered.

When she got home that night, she was able to tell her family about her experience.

Dan replied, 'I, for one want to see the movie. I can't even imagine what a thrill it was for you to sit there and watch the scenes enfold and to know from editing the book, exactly how it should have been enacted. How close do you feel they're following the book?'

'The two scenes I watched were almost identical to what I remember as being in the book' she confirmed.

'When will the movie be released?' Sandy asked. She was intrigued by it all and proud of her mom for having had a part in getting it made into a movie.

'They think it will be ready in about six months. The actual filming should be over in about three, but then they must edit it and move scenes around a bit until they're happy with it. They'll also have to add the music and voice-overs for some scenes. There are some parts where it will give Shirley's thoughts where you will just see Shirley standing or sitting there, but the voiceovers will be saying the words she's thinking. So, the female actor has to go to the studio and record those words.' Becky explained.

'It's really complicated, isn't it,' agreed Dan.

'Yes, but I can see why actors get a high acting in movies. It's a fantasy world, but in this case it's more like a nightmare world especially in the battering and wife abuse scenes. One feels that it's really happening, which was a bit scary, but the tension goes away immediately when the director says, 'Cut,' and the characters become themselves again. It was a bit spooky watching the man playing Shirley's husband talking calmly to the woman he supposedly just beat up. After that everyone relaxed and was able to get back to real life.'

Chapter 22

It was mid-August when Becky received a call from Brenda. She was talking so fast that Becky had to tell her to slow down.

'I just had to tell you first – well after I told Fred that is – she rambled on.'

'Had to tell me what? Did you get a new job or promotion?'

'No, silly! I phoned to tell you I'm pregnant!'

'You sound pretty stoked about it. What does Fred think?' Becky asked.

'He's so excited. He comes from a big family and has always talked to me about how much he wants kids. He has such a good job that we can afford to have one this early in our marriage. Oh, I'm so excited!' she prattled on.

'Do you want to borrow my maternity outfits when you start expanding?' Becky asked as she pictured Brenda's gorgeous figure being huge, but it was difficult to imagine it.

'Yeah – that would be nice. We both take about the same size, but you have more meat on your bones than me,' she added laughingly.

'Are you saying I'm fat!' insisted Becky.

'Oh no, just that you're much more curvaceous than I am,' she was quick to add.

'That's better. What are you hoping for – a boy or a girl?'

'I'm partial to having a girl, but don't really care.'

'Well, if it's a girl, I have a little tyke here that can pass down some outfits.'

'That would be great.'

They talked for quite a while about the wonders of motherhood, and when Becky invited them over for dinner, Dan shook Fred's hand and congratulated him.

When Brenda was in her third month, she had an ultrasound because the doctor felt she was gaining too much weight. As soon as she arrived home from her check-up – she phoned Becky.

'You're not going to believe this!' she almost shouted when Becky picked up the phone.

Becky recognized her voice, so knew it was something Brenda wanted to talk to her about.

'What happened?'

'I'm carrying twins! Can you believe that?'

'Wow. That's amazing.'

'Fred has twin brothers and two of his cousins are twins, so we should have expected this. But I have to tell you I'm overwhelmed with it all.'

'I don't blame you. I'd be flabbergasted if I was told I was carrying twins!' Becky agreed.

'The doctor suggested that I just work part-time for a couple of months then take time off after that, so I don't overstrain myself because of the extra weight I'll be carrying.'

'I can understand that. But can you imagine how big you'll get?' teased Becky.

'You had to say that didn't you. You're mean!' she said as she laughed. She was not looking forward to looking like a whale. Fred had shown her pictures of his mother when she was pregnant with his twin brothers and she was huge at seven months.

'Well, you take care of yourself and look after those little ones. No doing goofy stuff. You'll have to cut down on the number of workouts you do. I'm sure lifting weights etc. are not what you should be doing.'

'My doctor has given me a reduced exercise plan that will help me when I deliver. She doesn't want me to stop doing exercises; just to do less strenuous ones.'

'Well, I'm overjoyed by your news. I'll tell Dan when he comes home and I'm sure he'll be pleased as well.'

In June when Brenda was in her seventh month, everyone agreed that she was massive and could see that it was very difficult for her to get around. Most of her body was still slim looking, but the mound in front of her was so huge she hadn't seen her feet in a month. She now needed someone to help her put her shoes on and help her up from chairs and out of bed. That summer had been a scorcher so far, and she was really feeling the heat. It became necessary for her to lie down quite often just so she could breathe properly.

'I feel as if two pairs of feet are continually kicking me in my lungs. I can't seem to get enough air unless I'm lying down,' she panted. 'I have to use a pillow between my knees when I lie on my side and a pillow under my knees when I lie on my back - otherwise my back hurts. My God I can't take much more of this!' she lamented to Becky.

She was so uncomfortable most of the time, that she couldn't wait to deliver, but knew that every extra day she carried her babies would help them both survive. Fred's mother had delivered her twins in the middle of her seventh month, and Fred's aunt delivered her twins when she had almost made it into her eighth month. So, Brenda knew it was likely that she would have her babies soon.

When it was late May, and Brenda had successfully carried her babies for almost eight months, Fred called Becky at nine o'clock one morning to tell her that Brenda had been taken to the hospital at three that night and it wouldn't be long till the babies would arrive. They were pleased that she didn't seem to need a caesarean, and the babies were doing fine.

'I hate watching Brenda go through this. She's exhausted already,' he explained.

'Well, do keep me informed,' Becky requested.

'I'll do that. Now I'd better get back to her. I've just stepped outside to get a cup of coffee and thought I should phone her parents and knew you'd want to know as well.'

'Thanks Fred. Give Brenda my love.'

Two hours later Fred called to announce that he was now the father of identical female twins who had all their fingers and toes and were just as cute as a button.

'Congratulations. I guess it will be a few days until Brenda will come home after that ordeal. Will the twins have to stay in the hospital for extra days?'

'They think they'll be ready to go home when they're about a week old, so will only stay in a couple of extra days. Brenda is hoping to keep nursing them and will express her milk at home during the night.'

All went according to plan, and Becky was able to see the little girls a few days after they arrived home. She could see they were identical and wondered how Brenda could tell them apart.

'I can't tell them apart yet, so I've left the little hospital bracelets on them and added their names.'

'What did you call them?'

'We thought for a long time before we named them. It's a bit harder to pick out two names that go together. We've decided that one of them will be Jana Rebecca Connolly...'

Becky gasped, 'You named one of them after me?'

'Sure, you're my best friend and we debated whether we would call her Jana Becky Connolly, or the longer version of Jana Rebecca Connolly and we chose the second.'

'What did you call the second little darling?'

'Her name will be Jill Maria Connolly after Fred's mother Maria.'

'Sounds good' she agreed as she checked the names on the babies' wrists. 'So, this is the one with my name,' she said.

'Would you like to hold her?' Brenda asked.

'Sure would.' She picked up the baby from the little bed she shared with her sister and sat with her on the sofa examining her little fingers and toes. 'Jana and Jill are certainly going to grow up cute, because as infants they're absolutely precious,' she said to their proud mother.

'By the way, Sandy has offered to babysit if you need one. She'll be fifteen next month and has been babysitting for two years, so hopefully she could handle twins. Otherwise, maybe I could help and babysit.

'That would be great,' agreed Brenda.

Chapter 23

When the debut of Shirley's movie 'Broken Dreams' was offered to a select group of people in April, Jim Stevens and his entire staff were invited. Becky sat next to Shirley and held her hand as the credits rolled by giving Shirley credit for having written the book. Everyone at the premier was given a copy of the movie on DVD so they could view it again at home.

The movie was quite emotional, and several times Becky and Shirley had tears running down their cheeks as did many others watching the movie. When it was finished, the producer of the movie asked the audience to fill in the card they'd been given to evaluate the movie. He encouraged everyone to be honest in their evaluation.

After the premier, the producer spoke with Jim and told him that there was only one person in the audience who had anything negative to say. The man wrote that the movie was slanted too much in the woman's favour, that the husband had not been given a chance to tell his side of the story. Other than that, it was a rounding success and was released in Canada and the United States two weeks later and went world-wide the next month.

The sales were beyond even their expectations and Shirley became a rich woman. Some of her share of the royalties was given to Becky's publishing firm and in turn, Jim Stevens gave his staff bonuses from that money. He decided to give a double bonus to Becky because of the work she'd done to make the book and movie such a success.

Becky was excited when she got home from the meeting Jim had called for his staff and was pleased to tell her family that she wanted to use the money to take her family to Hawaii in June when school holidays began. In the meantime, they were kept busy updating their passports and getting one for both Mike and baby Vicki. It was hard to know what to take when travelling with two children who required special restraint seats but were happy to learn when they phoned Alamo Car rentals that they would be able to rent two of them when they rented the car on Maui.

It was quite an experience travelling with a teenager, a four-year-old boy and a toddler who had just learned how to walk. On the airplane, they decided to purchase the four inside seats of a row even though Mike wanted to have a window seat. Because Vicki was under one year of age, they did not have to buy a ticket for her. The airline advised that they would provide a crib that could be clipped to the wall in front of their first row of seats. However, because Vicki was now rather heavy, they decided that she should have a seat as well as having access to the crib.

As planned, as soon as they arrived in Honolulu, they boarded a plane for Maui, picked up their Alamo car with the children's car seats and drove across the island to the same hotel Becky and Dan had stayed in on their honeymoon. Mike and Vicki had not come on their earlier trip and Sandy was glad to be back where she could swim in the surf. She teased them when they got to their hotel, 'So this is where you spent your romantic honeymoon. I heard all about it!' she teased.

As before, they booked a hotel suite that had a kitchen and Sandy stayed with the two younger children while Becky and Dan went to stock up on the essentials they'd need. They'd decided that with three children, two of them quite little, it would be easier and more economical to eat many of their meals at home. They also planned on having picnics on the beach and had brought an insulated bag with them to hold those meals.

While at the airport, they'd picked up brochures about the sites they could visit on Maui and when Becky and Dan returned home from shopping and had their lunch the first day, they mulled over the choices offered to them. Sandy had been examining them while she waited for her parents to return from their shopping trip.

'Well, Sandy have you had a chance to examine the brochures?'

'Yes, I have. It looks like there are some great places to go. Which ones did you go to when you were here before?' she asked.

'I'd like to go back to the Tropical Fruit Plantation. We really enjoyed it when we were here on our Honeymoon.' Becky said.

'That sounds like a good place for all of us to go,' agreed Dan.

'There's one trip we won't take this time and that's for us to go up to Haleakala National Park,' said Becky.

'Aw Mom, that's one of the places I really wanted to see. Can't we go to see the volcano?' Sandy begged

'Well Mike and Vicki can't go – they're too little to do that.' Becky said sadly.

'I could take Sandy,' said Dan.

'Would you?' begged Sandy. 'I really want to go there.'

'Okay, but you realize that we have to get up really early in the morning, because the best way to see it is at sunrise. And it will be very cold up there as well.'

'I don't have any warm clothes,' Sandy said sadly, then as she read more information from the brochure said, 'Oh, look, it says they'll supply parkas for those who need them, so maybe we can go there one day.'

'Let's book it,' agreed Dan.

Sandy read more from the brochure and read it out to them, 'It says it's an old crater and adds you haven't experienced

Haleakala until you've seen it at sunrise on a Haleakala Crater Sunrise Tour. It offers breathtaking views of Maui at sunrise and includes a scenic drive through the Kula District and Puu Ulaula Overlook. It also says it has a professionally narrated tour with pick-up and drop-off at Maui hotels.'

Then Dan added, 'Here's another one we should book. Your Mom and I went on it and I know I'd like to do it again. How about a Molokini sail and Snorkel Adventure? It says, 'Cruise to Molokini and snorkel into a crescent-shaped submerged volcanic crater. Discover the beautiful coral reefs and tropical fish underneath the water or bask in the warmth of paradise. From the experienced snorkeler to those who cannot swim, this adventure is perfect for everyone - guaranteeing fun in the water or on the sundeck. The tour departure point in Maalaea Harbor is an easy 20-minute drive from Lahaina and Kahului. You will cruise along the Maui coastline and soak in the picturesque scenery and view the underwater sights from the glass-bottom viewing room and enjoy a complimentary breakfast and lunch,' Dan concluded.

'I'm sure Mike and Vicki would enjoy looking out the glass-bottom viewing room even though they're too young to snorkel.' Becky added.

'That sounds great. Why don't we book those three events, but leave the extra days just to enjoy lying on the beach and doing our own thing?' Becky suggested.

'Mom, I'm really anxious to go to the beach now that we're here. Can we go this afternoon?' Sandy begged.

Becky knew that the children would love going to the beach, and remembered one area along the shore where there was a little pool that formed after the tide went out that would be perfect for Vicki and Mike to paddle in. She reminded Dan of that location and suggested that he could possibly take Mike into the waves with him if they weren't too high.

Before they left for the beach, Dan called the tour companies and booked the three adventures.

When they got to the beach Mike was bug eyed as he watched the waves roll onto the beach. He'd never been to a beach before and started heading straight for the waves. Dan grabbed him saying, 'Oh no you don't little man! You have no idea how powerful those waves are. Here is where I want you to swim until you get used to the water.'

Mike pouted, but when he saw the little lake that was there, he first touched it with his foot. 'It's nice and warm,' he said, then ran right in. It was a very shallow pool that was formed every time the tide receded but warmed up quite nicely during the day. They had brought a sand pail and shovel and he was kept busy making sand castles. Becky kept a close watch over him and sat on the side of the pool with Vicki who laughed out loud as she splashed in the pool. She loved it when she splashed and got her mother wet and of course Becky pretended to be surprised every time it happened.

Dan and Sandy in the meantime were diving into the waves. Because Dan was a certified SCUBA diver like his brother Steve, he was very comfortable in the water, but stayed close and kept a watchful eye on Sandy as she dove into the waves. They had bought a little Styrofoam body board for Sandy to try out in the waves, and she was soon having a ball riding the waves.

Becky had insisted that they all wear long-sleeved light-weight tops and hats and had liberally covered them with sunscreen, knowing how easy it would be for them to get burned. She was sad when she had to insist that Mike and Vicki come away from the water and sit under the shade of a tree. Mike didn't want to leave the water and kicked up a fuss until Becky suggested that they look in the insulated bag to see if there was something he could drink. He was soon having his favourite bottle of juice while Vicki had a drink from her sippy cup. Vicki's eyes began to droop, and she soon fell asleep. By this time Dan and Sandy had returned and Becky put her finger to her lip to warn them to be quiet. They all enjoyed a drink, but Mike was restless.

Dan suggested, 'Hey Mike. Would you like to go for a walk along the beach? There are lots of shells you can gather.'

Mike was up like a shot, and Dan grabbed his sand pail to put the shells in.

'Can I come too,' asked Sandy. She too wanted to gather some shells to take back to her friends.

When they returned, everyone agreed it was time to go back to the hotel. Vicki was still sound asleep, and Dan gently secured her in her car seat, and she didn't wake up when he placed her in her little bed at the hotel.

They were all tired, and soon everyone had an afternoon nap. It was about six o'clock when they woke up. Becky felt a little groggy from having a sleep at such a time, but soon prepared a cold dinner of sliced ham, tomatoes and salad ready for everyone. After dinner was over, Dan asked his family, 'Who would like to have an ice cream cone?'

Of course, they all agreed, so off they went to the Dairy Queen for a treat.

The next day they all thoroughly enjoyed the Tropical Fruit Plantation and came away with a basket full of ripe fruit. Mike loved the fresh pineapple, and Sandy tried an avocado which she'd never tasted before. Dan bought flower leis for Sandy and Becky. They both loved the smell of the white and yellow frangipani flowers.

Sandy and Dan found that getting up so early for their trip to Haleakala National Park was a chore, but when they saw the sunset from the peak, they both felt it was worth the effort. Sandy found it very cold and snuggled down in her borrowed parka. She also realized that she was rather breathless and asked Dan about it.

'Your mom got quite breathless up here as well. It's because of the altitude That's why I didn't want to bring Mike and Vicki with us,' he explained.

On the Saturday night, Dan asked Sandy if she felt up to babysitting Mike and Vicki because he wanted to take their mom out for dinner.

'Sure, Dad. You guys need a romantic night out,' she teased.

He gave her a gentle swat on her shoulder. 'Thanks kiddo. I'll bring you back a milkshake when we get home.'

'Me too!' Mike insisted.

'Okay pal, when we get home, I'll wake you up and give you the milkshake.'

Becky fussed over her appearance. She remembered how romantic it had been when they'd been there on her honeymoon and hoped they could capture the feeling again.

She put on her lei that looked nice against the tan she'd acquired since coming to Hawaii. Dan wore a nice short-sleeved shirt and light-weight dress pants and for the first time wore shoes instead of sandals.

'You look yummy tonight,' he said as he seated her in the car.

'You look pretty yummy yourself,' she replied.

They enjoyed a lovely meal of mahi mahi fish and salad and topped it off sharing a piece of pecan pie. As they sat drinking their coffee, Becky said, 'I love this place. I still remember how lovely a time we had on our first trip here. You were so romantic, and we made love so many times on our honeymoon that we had to force ourselves to go on the tours. This time, it's been different, but nice having the kids with us. We do make a nice family group, don't we?' she said as she took his hand.

'The best! How did we luck out finding each other, and having such good kids? I'm so glad we had Vicki because she's a part of both of us, but I feel as close to Sandy as if she had been born to me. I have to admit that I don't see much of Ken because he's working in Edson, but he's grown up to be a very nice young man.'

'And I feel the same way about Mike. He's fitted well into our family and I miss him the weeks he's with Emily and Al. It's so nice that you have such a good relationship with Emily, and it was nice of her to invite us to their wedding. Not many ex-spouses would have done that.'

'You're right. We're a very lucky couple. I love my job as a detective, and I know you enjoy yours looking after your authors and are looking forward to editing Shirley's next book. And I know you love your volunteering work with Crime Stoppers. What more could we want?' he said as he hugged her to him.

'Yes, life is wonderful,' she agreed.

****

I hope you enjoyed this second book in a series of books about Becky, Dan, and their families. The first in the series was entitled:

Twists and Turns

There will be more books about this family to come.

Roberta Cava

www.ingramcontent.com/pod-product-compliance
Lightning Source LLC
Chambersburg PA
CBHW070930250626
47159CB00009B/3193